THE GENIE OF SUTTON PLACE

BY GEORGE SELDEN

GEORGE SELDEN Thompson

THE GENIE OF SUTTON PLACE

Farrar, Straus and Giroux : New York

For Edward J. Czerwinski,
who is something of a genie,
in his accomplishments, himself

CONTENTS

THE GENIE OF SUTTON PLACE

1

A Bad Beginning

"Even great deeds that are done by magic can be forgotten utterly."

At least that's what Dooley says. He says that he's even beginning to forget the times when he worked for the Master of Magic himself. Humanity taking over, I guess. And of course Sam is only too glad to forget his past. That's humanity again, and very natural in the case of Sam. Aunt Lucy and Rose don't have anything to remember. They never even suspected what was going on right under their noses. I hate to admit it, after all the excitement of everything, but I'm getting a little fuzzy on the details myself. We human beings are mostly just forgetful, that's all. And unobservant and pretty unbelieving, too, a lot of the time . . . But Dooley says, with that secret smile of his, we have "many subtle compensations."

It was Dooley who suggested I write it all down. It does seem a long time ago now! That must be the magic. It makes everything feel unreal. But the whole thing happened just this summer, right here in New York.

I guess the beginning was one morning in June. A very gloomy beginning, too, despite how bright and sunshiny the day was outside. I was still feeling depressed and angry and lonely about Lorenzo's death. He was my father. (I *did* believe he was dead, though; it took me weeks just to get that far.) And when Madame Sosostris happened to mention, with a phony light tone in her voice, that Aunt Lucy and her lawyer were dropping down that morning to see me, my suspicions got nervous.

"What are they dropping down about?" I wanted to know.

"Oh—just something to do with Lorenzo's will," said Madame Sosostris, with a casual wave of her hand that made me feel as if I'd been whacked on the head.

"And that's all? Just the will?" I said.

"Well, I think your aunt said something about your future, too."

That did it. Doomsville! When a kid hears that grown-ups are going to discuss "his future," he'd better watch out. Especially if he's had as much fun in his past as I did down in Greenwich Village with Lorenzo and Madame Sosostris.

For an hour or so I moped around the shop, pretending to examine the new consignment that had come in the day before, but really just waiting for my "future" to be discussed. You see, the front room of Madame Sosostris's apartment is her antique shop. She calls it her junk shop, but that's really not right. She has a great eye for furniture and objects and things, and although her shop is one of the smallest in the Village, it's also one of the best. The antiques are how she supports herself—and me and Lorenzo, too, when we lived down there. But her real passion is in the back room, with the big round table and all the supernatural gadgets. That's where she holds her séances and gets in touch with the Spirit World. Or at least *tries* to get in touch. Boy, does she ever try!

So I was walking around, looking at all the new things, and Sam was padding after me. Sam was my dog. You're going to hear a lot about him. He was a mongrel. It turned out that he was half basset hound and half springer spaniel. But that comes later. We didn't know that then.

It gives you some idea of his size, though. Pretty big. He was always bumping up against chair legs in that cluttered antique shop, and a couple of times he broke some things, too. But in all the five years that he was my pet, Madame Sosostris never scolded him once. Not even the time when he knocked over the crystal candlestick. She knew how much I loved him, and that's just the kind of woman she is.

Sam knew something was wrong that day. When a dog has a boy as long as Sam had me, they get to know each other pretty well. Even when I stopped to look at the antique American bull's-eye mirror, he knew I was faking enthusiasm. It was the kind of mirror that has the curved glass in which you can see a whole room, and the gold frame, and the eagle on top, and I've always had a thing about them. But I couldn't fool Sam. He waddled up and put his head against my leg, and his hangdog expression hung down even further. You know what basset hounds look like.

"That's a beauty, isn't it, Tim?" said Madame Sosostris. I nodded. "Sure is."

"I think maybe it's time you had one of those mirrors for your own."

"Let's just wait and see what happens," I said, hoping that what was going to happen wouldn't start right away.

But it did. Just then Aunt Lucy, Henry Watkins, her lawyer, and Maurice, the chauffeur, drove up in that big car that Aunt Lucy didn't like at all. She admitted it to me later when Dooley and I persuaded her to get a new little one. She didn't much like Maurice either, although she'd never admit that. But she inherited him, along with the big car, from Grampa Lorenzo, Lorenzo's father. I'd seen Maurice a few times before, up in Aunt Lucy's apartment in Sutton Place. The thing I remember most about him is his mouth. It was always tightened up, as if there was a string in his lips that pulled them together like a lady's purse. Oh, and I remember he called Aunt Lucy "modom." I think it's pretty silly to call a woman "madame" anyway, unless you live in France perhaps. But Maurice didn't even call her that. He called her "modom," and his mouth would end up all puckered together.

Now, about Aunt Lucy. The best way to describe Aunt Lucy is to show you Madame Sosostris first—because they were opposites. To begin with, Madame Sosostris wasn't Madame Sosostris. Her real name was Muriel Glicker. But one day she and Lorenzo and I were sitting around reading poetry out loud. We read a lot of poetry together on rainy days. And on this particular day we were reading a poem called *The Waste Land*. It's a very good poem, too. And in it the author talks about someone named Madame Sosostris. Well, when Madame Sosostris heard that name, she jumped up from her chair, smacked her forehead, and said, "That's me!" From then on she was

known to *everybody* as Madame Sosostris. Because that's
who she *was*! That same afternoon she tie-dyed a dishtowel and whipped it up into the best-looking turban this
side of Baghdad. (Dooley agrees. He knows, too, about
turbans and pantaloons and things like that.) And she
changed the name of her shop from Muriel's Antiques to
Madame Sosostris: Medium and Antique Dealer. Lorenzo
and I helped her make the new sign. She said that she'd
always felt that her most important work was in the Occult
Sciences, not the high-class junk out front. And as for the
turban, that just meant that she didn't have to keep dyeing
her hair that awful red color. She said, "Let it go gray,
and the hell with it!"

But Aunt Lucy . . . There are some people who don't
look at home in their names. Not their real names, nor
the names they invent for themselves. And Aunt Lucy
was one. Her real name was Lucy Farr. Which I think is
pretty nice. You know—Farr, distance, horizons, all that.
But Aunt Lucy had no sense of horizons. To begin with,
at least. She's short, and I think it bothered her. I mean,
there's nothing wrong with being short. I'm short, too. Of
course I'm thirteen, just barely, so I'm supposed to still
be short. Lorenzo was short, and he said that my mother,
who died when I was too little to remember, was also a
very small person. Except I may remember her. There
was a night, which I think was real, with the moon and

street lights and a few bright stars—and somebody was holding me. So there's nothing wrong with being short.

But Aunt Lucy made you feel as if there was. Everything she wore was long. Her necklaces, her earrings, the works. It all was supposed to make you think she was long and tall herself. And her clothes were another thing that was wrong. Madame Sosostris could look great in a tie-dyed dishtowel and a pair of old Levi's, but Aunt Lucy's clothes never worked together. If her blouse was one color, her skirt would be exactly the color that fought with the blouse. And you knew just to look at her that everything she wore cost a fortune. It's a funny thing about money, though. It doesn't do you a bit of good unless you know where to spend it.

There are some people who just need help in living, and Aunt Lucy was one. (She was going to *get* help, too— but from someone nobody'd ever suspect.)

As for Mr. Watkins—well, I don't have anything against lawyers, but when he marched into the antique shop, with that dark gray suit and pinstripe shirt and black briefcase, I sort of wished he'd been one of the bearded hippies that drop in to browse around instead.

Madame Sosostris said hello to everybody, and then, after a few minutes of nobody knowing what more to say, Mr. Watkins spoke up. "I guess we'd better get down to business." He glanced around, and his nose kind of crinkled. "Pretty crowded in here. Have you a place where we could all sit down, Madame Sosostris?"

"Sure. The séance table in the back room," said Madame S.

We left Maurice outside, leaning against the fender of Aunt Lucy's car. A crowd of neighborhood kids was beginning to collect to gawk at them, because you don't see a car like that *or* a chauffeur in a uniform very often in that part of Greenwich Village.

Madame Sosostris led the way to the back. Sam and I came last. Usually Sam gets just as excited as I do when we go to the séance table. His tail wags like mad. That's how he broke the candlestick. But it wasn't wagging now.

The good times we've had at that big round séance table!—with the dark maroon cover over it and the Tiffany lamp hanging down from two of Lorenzo's neckties, because we kept forgetting to get a new chain. All those magical colors in the glass! Like the fun when the Willy sisters came each month . . . I only wished we were going to have a séance now.

2

More of the Same

"I think we might proceed," began Mr. Watkins in a voice that sounded just the way his gray suit looked, "with the reading of the will of the late—"

Just then Sam, who was blobbing around under the table looking for a place to lie down amid all our feet, happened to step on the Lulu button and interrupted the reading of the will of the late my father. A white shape shot out of a compartment in the wall above Madame Sosostris's head and hung there, shivering.

"Good Lord—what's that?" exclaimed Aunt Lucy.

"Excuse it, please." Madame Sosostris stood up. "It's just Lulu, my ghost." She put Lulu, who was a piece of sheet attached to the end of a spring, back into the wall.

Mr. Watkins interrupted the reading again to ask, "Have you ever gotten a *real* ghost, Madame Sosostris?" His nose crinkled once more, skeptically.

"Not yet, Mr. Watkins," said Madame Sosostris. She wasn't angry either, the way she could have been. She just went on to explain reasonably, "But I will. I know Lulu here is a fake, but how I feel is, if the real Spirits know that I'm on their side—and Lulu shows I am—then sooner or later they'll show themselves to me in person."

"I see," said Mr. Watkins. "Then Lulu might be said to be bait for the spirits."

"That's exactly right!" She didn't get it that Mr. Watkins was making fun of her. Madame Sosostris is a serious medium. She may read a palm now and then, but she doesn't do dopey things like feeling the bumps on a person's head to tell his future, or—worst of all, like some fakes—reading the soles of a person's feet.

"I'll go on with the reading of the will of the late Lorenzo Farr. He died, as we all know—and rather needlessly, I'm afraid—"

Daddy died when the tomb he was excavating collapsed on him. He was looking for some very important inscriptions. And it was *not* needless! Archaeology is important.

"—in an unfortunate accident in Mesopotamia. I now read his will. 'I, Lorenzo Farr, being of sound mind and body—' " His nose did its thing.

Now I have to interrupt the reading myself. And tell you about Lorenzo. A lot of people did think he was *not* of sound mind. Although everyone would have to agree that his body, though small, was strong, and his face was happy and handsome, too. The reason people like Mr. Watkins sniff when they talk about Lorenzo is that after working five years with Grampa Lorenzo, getting ready to inherit the business, Lorenzo just quit and began to study the Occult Sciences. That's what he'd been interested in all along. Of course nowadays everybody "drops out." It's the thing to do. But I remember one day when Lorenzo and Madame Sosostris and I were making pancakes, and Lorenzo said, "I'm the original dropout." And Madame Sosostris—it was the Occult Sciences, a mutual interest, that brought them together—said, "Lorenzo, you didn't drop out, you dropped *in*! Right into just what you wanted to do. I hope it sets a trend." It may have, too.

Mr. Watkins went on with the reading. " '—do hereby declare that this is my last will and testament. In recognition of our many years of friendship and her continuous help and kindness in rearing my young son, Timothy, I leave to my colleague Madame Sosostris my Ummayad

astrolabe—' " That's something for figuring out the stars.
The Ummayads were a dynasty of Arab kings. Lorenzo
was very interested in everything Arabian. Thank goodness! " '—and my Tang dynasty divining rod—' " That
came from China—" 'knowing how much she has always
admired these instruments and hoping that they may
assist her in every possible way.' "

Right there Madame Sosostris began to cry, but quietly.
I'm glad she did, too. The reading of a will is a sad time,
and I didn't want to start crying, too.

Mr. Watkins went on: " 'To my son, Timothy, I leave
all the rest of my worldly goods, which consist chiefly of
my books, the priceless records of many years devoted to
the pursuit of the Occult Sciences. They contain many
wonders and may provide unexpected assistance for him.' "

I almost stopped feeling sad when I heard that.
Lorenzo's books were *mine*! Oh, those books! They were
up on shelves all around the séance room. Hundreds! And
they ranged all the way from fictional ghost stories to very
serious scientific stuff—way over my head—like the
studies in extrasensory perception that they're doing down
at Duke University. In between there were medieval trea-
tises on alchemy, and German studies of poltergeists, and
French books about possession, and most valuable of all—
Lorenzo's diary of the years he spent traveling in Europe
after he dropped out of Grampa Lorenzo's business. Even
if I didn't get a lot of what was in those books, they've

always been magical for me. It made my heart jiggle to browse through them.

More reading: " 'I wish that I had a larger legacy to bequeath to my son, since among all the discoveries I have made, the most marvelous, most magical, and the best beloved has been Timothy himself.' "

At this point I was bawling along with Madame Sosostris. Aunt Lucy was sitting next to me, and she reached out and took my hand. It was awkward, the way she did it—she didn't know how to squeeze hands yet—but she meant well, anyway.

" 'To my sister, Lucy, whom—to my sorrow—I've seen so little in recent years, I leave my love, undiminished since our childhood—' " I think Lorenzo put that in because he wanted Aunt Lucy to know that he didn't stop loving her just because Grampa Lorenzo disinherited him when he left the business and left all the money and the Sutton Place apartment and the car and Maurice to her when he died—" 'and I also leave the heartfelt wish that, should anything befall me, she may watch over my boy and stand in the place of a parent to him.' "

I was assuming that meant she would keep me in food and clothes, but it brought another squeeze from Aunt Lucy.

" 'Finally,' " Mr. Watkins concluded, " 'to Timmy I also leave the custody of our dear friend Sam—' " Under the table, when he heard his own name, Sam began to wag his tail on my foot. I looked down, and Sam was smiling. Some dogs *can* smile, you know—grin, sort of—and Sam's smile, in its own animal way, was just as beautiful as Dooley's—" 'a soul so dear to my young son, and so loving, that I am inclined to the view that in some previous incarnation he was much more than a dog to him.' Well, really!" Mr. Watkins took off his spectacles, readjusted his nose, and began to put his papers back into his briefcase. That "well, really" was pure Watkins and *not* from my father's will.

Aunt Lucy bumbled into the silence that followed. "Uh —is that all?"

"I should think that was quite enough!" said Mr. Watkins. But then he got hooked on the humanity in him, too. He saw the bad shape that I still was in, his eyes kind of winced, and he said, "You're a very lucky young lady, Lucy, to gain the custody of such a handsome chap. Considering the bizarre upbringing he's had."

Now, about my "bizarre upbringing"—before I tell you how that word "custody" dried my eyes like fire and made me begin to panic . . .

My years up to then were things like these. On a day last January it was snowing outside. Suddenly Lorenzo threw down his copy of *The New York Times* and shouted, "Okay! Everybody into heavy clothes! We're going bicycle riding!" Madame Sosostris and I groaned, "No!" but we knew it wouldn't do any good. When Lorenzo got enthused like that, there wasn't any stopping him. So out we went and wheeled around the Battery and all lower Manhattan. While the snow wheeled around the three of us. Then —Lorenzo must have guessed it was ending—while everyone else was getting up the energy to shovel their sidewalks, the sun came out in the last part of the afternoon, and we had the whole white world to ourselves.

And another time, two summers ago: one hot August morning we were all getting ready to go to the beach when Lorenzo decided, "Nope! The National Museum!" I was really mad that time, because I *do* like to swim. But by the end of the afternoon, by the time Lorenzo had talked the guard into letting us stay an extra ten minutes in the Near Eastern wing, I'd forgotten all about the beach . . . To think, we were right next to the room of rooms— the Al-Hazred room . . . If I'd known that then . . .

One more thing only—and not magic or kooky bicycle riding either. It's how I learned to cook. One night Lorenzo said, "I'd like some pancakes." Naturally I said, "So would I." "Then go make them," said Lorenzo. "There's a cook book over the kitchen sink." So, to my nervousness, I did. And, believe me, they were *awful*! Much too thick and starchy. For the first batch Lorenzo and Madame Sosostris had to pretend like mad. Then he took over, and none of us had to pretend at all.

So if that's a "bizarre upbringing," I just wish everybody could enjoy their own as much.

But all the time those good memories of Lorenzo were
going through my mind, warming it up, that word "custody" was in there, too, freezing it! Custody is something
orphans and criminals get taken into. I don't know how a
criminal feels when he hears he's in custody, but *I* knew
the worst. Nobody said anything, but all of a sudden the
séance room was full of the fact that I was going to have
to leave Madame Sosostris and go live with Aunt Lucy.

At first I was just plain scared, and I tried to think how
I could stop it all from happening. No way. I was going
to say something dopey, like that Daddy had said I should
take care of Madame Sosostris while he was away excavating, and that she should take care of me—but no way. I
gave up on all that and started to be rational and cook up
a reason to come down and see Madame Sosostris. Every
day, if I could.

While I was plotting what I thought was a pretty good
idea, the others were talking. I half-heard Aunt Lucy say
something about how fortunate it was that the school year
had just ended, so that I'd have the summer before beginning a new school in the fall.

Madame Sosostris shot me a glance—half worry and
half fun—and said, "Oh, Tim's very bright. He won't have
any trouble." She knew I hadn't been to school for ages.
It was so dull, and the things I was learning there were
so stupid that I just sort of phased out about two years

ago. That's when my education began. "He can even read Latin," said Madame Sosostris.

"Why, that's wonderful!" exclaimed Aunt Lucy.

One day Lorenzo was translating a juicy section from a treatise on alchemy by Paracelsus. Abruptly he stopped and said, "There's no reason why I should be doing this." That minute he started to teach me Latin.

"Darn good at arithmetic, too!" said Madame Sosostris.

She and Lorenzo had had to go to an auction, and as they were going out the door, she casually called back, "Mind the store, Tim." By the time they got back, I could make change like anything. And that involves addition, subtraction, and all that stuff. I was lucky, though, that afternoon. We had very nice customers and nobody tried to gyp me.

"Has he been exposed to the new math?" said Mr. Watkins.

I was going to say that as a matter of fact I hadn't been exposed to the new math, but I'd had on-the-job training in finance and economics, but I decided he'd just think that I was some smarty-pants kid, so I shut up.

The talk hemmed and hawed for a while longer, and then there came a dead moment when everyone knew it was time for me and Aunt Lucy and Mr. Watkins to leave.

"Well, Timmy, I think perhaps you'd better get your things," Aunt Lucy said quietly.

"All right," I answered, very cool. Because by then I

had my plan. I went up to my bedroom and packed.

It's very hard to describe my bedroom down there, because it never stayed the same. The only things that didn't change were the bed and the bookcase. All the rest of the furniture was things that Madame Sosostris didn't have room for yet in the shop downstairs. And when she did—a new table, a new chair, a new everything! I liked it. The changes made life interesting.

I stuffed my clothes in my suitcase and put my two favorite kids' books on top of them: *The Hobbit* and *The Wizard of Oz*. I was sure I could take at least them without interfering with the plan. Then I went downstairs.

Oh—very important—I also brought the Good-Luck Devil from Borneo—a little statuette with a fierce but intelligent face. He certainly didn't live up to his reputation for bringing good luck, but I loved him and I wanted him with me.

Everybody was in that dithery state when you're getting ready to say goodbye. A good time to spring my idea, I decided. "Madame Sosostris," I said, "would you mind if I left Lorenzo's books down here for a while? There's really an awful lot of them, and I don't know whether they'd fit in Aunt Lucy's apartment."

"Why, I've plenty of room—" Aunt Lucy began.

But Madame Sosostris, who caught on right away, interrupted. "Sure, Tim. As a matter of fact, I'd like to look them over myself. And if you ever want one," she added nonchalantly, "you can come down and pick it up any time. That would be okay with you, Miss Farr, wouldn't it?—not to have these dusty old books around?"

With many nods and smiles—especially between me and Madame S.—it all was agreed upon. So at least the plan worked.

Then the march through the shop to the car began.

Except that Sam, being his bumbly self in those days, had to interrupt it. At the door to the séance room he stepped on another button. The Fiendish Laughter rang out—pretty squawkily, I thought. Madame Sosostris apologized, and received a sniff and an understanding smile from Mr. Watkins and Aunt Lucy.

Sam's setting off the Fiendish Laughter made Mr. Watkins edgy. He said to Aunt Lucy, in the voice that grownups use when they don't want to be overheard by children, even when the child is standing right there beside them, "You are really going to take that mutt up to your apartment, Lucy?"

And Aunt Lucy, in the same fake voice, said, "Well, of course, Henry. It's his *dog*!"

The things that grownups don't know. Kids listen. And they *think*.

We arrived at the car. Maurice opened the door officiously.

We pretended we were cool and easy, but all of us knew we were all uptight . . .

The best thing was to get it over with quickly.

I said, "Madame Sosostris, you better get some new Fiendish Laughter. The old laughter's wearing out."

At that point so was mine.

3

Worse Yet

The drive uptown to Sutton Place took nearly an hour. Traffic. I love New York, but I hate the cars. But what is New York without the cars? . . . It's a problem for everybody, I guess.

The three of us were sitting in the back seat—Sam, Aunt Lucy, and me. I sat in the middle and let Sam have the window, because I knew he was going to enjoy the ride a lot more than I was. Mr. Watkins was up front with Maurice. He said he was going to "jump off" at his office on Third Avenue and Forty-first Street. Their two heads looked sort of alike up there.

I kept paying attention to Aunt Lucy's chatter—like about how little luggage I had—and remembering to answer her, but my arm was around Sam as he gazed out the window. Every now and then he'd give a little reverse push of his back and a woof to let me know that he knew I was there, despite how much he was enjoying the sights. I liked feeling his back underneath my hand. Sam was a husky mutt, and maybe a little overweight, but I'd rather have dogs—and people, too—have a bit too much stomach than be scrawny and not have enough.

So we let Mr. Watkins "jump off," and finally got to Sutton Place. Maurice let us out in front of Aunt Lucy's apartment house and told "modom" he'd return the car to the garage.

About Sutton Place. I don't have anything against it. A lot of rich people live there, but the buildings are pretty nice. There are old buildings and new ones, and a few really great town houses, but the whole place really does fit together. Aunt Lucy's apartment house was neither young nor old, but it had a nice big lobby, and the doorman was neither young nor old, but he, too, looked pretty permanent. So with everything so—acceptable—to say the least, I kept wondering why I felt so lousy on the elevator up to Aunt Lucy's apartment. I really was trying to psych myself into liking it all. But it didn't work.

And the reason it didn't, besides losing everything I was used to, was my bedroom. I knew the apartment already, from my visits with Lorenzo, and I appreciated it. Grampa Lorenzo's stuff, which Aunt Lucy didn't dare change, was like Sutton Place: old and new, and all good. A bull's-eye mirror would have fitted in very well. But then Aunt Lucy, with a grin out of a store window, said, "Now come and see *your* room, Timmy!"

She'd had the guest bedroom redecorated. And, boy, was it ever decorated! The trouble was, I didn't think the decorator knew anything about kids—much less me. I could have been four—or eighteen. Half the room was college pennants, and the other half was cuddly stuffed animals! And the worst—the most unbelievable thing—there weren't any bookcases in it! How can anybody design a room for a kid and not put at least one bookcase in it?

"Look, Timmy," said Aunt Lucy. "You open these cabinet doors, and there's *color* television!"

I'm not underestimating color television. A lot of kids would sell their souls for it. And some of the programs are pretty good, too.

"It's very nice, Aunt Lucy," I said.

"But, oh, dear, I'm afraid I've forgotten to include a doghouse for Sam."

"Aunt Lucy," I said, "Sam doesn't need anything but a piece of floor to lie down on." (Actually, he had his box. Which I went down and got in a couple of days.)

At that moment Sam was up on top of my chintz-covered bed, sniffing a Princeton flag. He was always able to enjoy things more easily than I could.

"Well, that's fine," said Aunt Lucy. "Just fine. I'll leave you two to make yourselves at home." She was just as uptight as I was, and she beat a retreat to her own bedroom.

That was the worst—when Sam and I were alone in "*my* room." It was even more lonely than "custody" down in Madame Sosostris's séance room.

I guess Sam wasn't as down as I was, though. He kept me company for a while and then padded off down the hall. (It's pretty clear, considering all the trouble that came later, that he was following the trail of perfume Aunt Lucy left in the air on the way to her bedroom.)

So there I was, all by myself, staring at a color TV set that I didn't want to turn on, with even Sam deserting me.

But I wasn't alone for long. Because just then Rose Jackson came in. Rose is one of those people who, when they come into a room—even an awful one like my bedroom—make everything feel more natural. More human, I mean.

"Hi," she said. "I hear you're going to live with us."

"I guess I am," I admitted.

"Come on in the kitchen. Let's have a Coke and get acquainted," said Rose.

Rose is Aunt Lucy's sleep-in maid, housekeeper, and cook. (Maurice, by the way, slept out. Which was going to make things easier.) Rose really is a singer, although she doesn't know yet whether she's a true dramatic soprano or a mezzo. She works for Aunt Lucy to pay for her music lessons, and part of the deal is that she can vocalize in her own bedroom as much as she likes. There's nothing wrong with being a maid, and if that's what you want, I'm all for it, but believe me, Rose Jackson is a girl who's *not* ever going to be satisfied with only washing dishes. And she's twenty-two. I found out all that while she found out all about me when we were having our Cokes in the kitchen. Rose was doing her favorite hobby as we talked, filling in a cross-word puzzle.

About this time on that first afternoon, I was beginning to think that Sutton Place was a place where you could feel at home.

But the feeling didn't last long. Aunt Lucy came brisking into the kitchen, patted her leg to summon someone, and said in a very persnickety way, "Come, Sam. Come, Sam. Sam, *come*!" Then after Sam had plopped in, she looked at me with a smile that if it had been glass could easily have been broken and said in the same kind of voice, "I *love* having you here to live with me, Timmy—but there's one thing we have to have clear. Sam's *not* to follow me around! And he's not to come into my bedroom. All right?"

"All right, Aunt Lucy," I said.

Rose said softly, "Come on, Sam—over here." And Sam went to her hand. But he kept looking back at Aunt Lucy. Rose flicked me a glance that advised me not to start worrying—yet. Like me, she always knew right away when everything was *not* all right.

The trouble was, Sam just downright fell in love with Aunt Lucy. It was love at first sight and love at first whiff of her beautiful perfume. A lot of it was my fault. I left them alone together.

You see, I had this scheme. As long as I was going to have to live in my bedroom, I wanted to make it as friendly as I could. I asked Aunt Lucy if she'd care if I made a few changes in it. She said, Why, dear, of course not!—not knowing at all what I had in mind. So little by little I began to take things out of my bedroom and down to the antique shop. It gave me an excuse to see Madame Sosostris every day, too. Even better than the books.

By the end of a couple of weeks I'd gotten rid of the college banners, the cutesy cushions, and the worst of the pictures. They were a series of framed illustrations from a really rotten children's book—about this courageous little boy who overcame some dopey phony handicap—and they must have cost Aunt Lucy a fortune. Of course Madame Sosostris wouldn't sell junk like that in her shop, but she palmed them off on some of her less intelligent colleagues.

Instead of that junk, I'd smuggled up to Sutton Place my big Bavarian pipe with the bowl in the shape of a skull, my fake mummy's hand—you can love a fake, it just has to be real—and, best of all, my bone. One day Lorenzo and I had discovered this strange bone inside an Aztec urn. Well, it could have been anything. It could have been from a dinosaur or it could have been—I won't even hope what. But I wanted it for my own. And since there was no retail value in it, Madame Sosostris gave it to me. My favorite was still the Good-Luck Devil from Borneo, but he looked much more at home with my other things all there, too.

Oh, I also bought a couple of little bookcases from the shop next to ours. That day I had to take a taxi, to get them back. If I'd known what was going to happen, I'd have taken a taxi—and Sam—every day. But Lorenzo had trained me to save money—we never had much—so I'd walk over to Third Avenue and take the E train down to the Village. You can't take dogs on the subway, unless they're in a box or something. Or unless you're blind. Sam was much too big for me to carry in a box.

But that meant that all the time I was schlepping everything around, Sam was left up in Sutton Place. And he was bugging Aunt Lucy. I didn't really know how much till the day she blew up. Then Rose told me . . .

I guess that you can love somebody and still be a terrible nuisance to them . . .

Rose told me that that hassle in the kitchen on my first day was just the beginning. Of course, Rose has a great sense of humor, so she could see the funniness of it in spite of Aunt Lucy's explosion. The time she got the biggest kick, she said, was when Aunt Lucy was getting ready to go out to lunch with Mr. Watkins. She'd just gotten out of the shower, and was dressing and primping, with Rose helping her, telling her how pretty she looked.

"Then all of a sudden we heard this pitiful woof from the doorway," said Rose, through her laughing. "And there was Sam, looking even more moony than usual." You know that a dog who turns out to be half basset hound looks pretty soulful anyway. "Your aunt acted as if poor old Sam was a peeping Tom."

A few of these embarrassing moments I saw myself, but I didn't put them all together. Like the time Aunt Lucy was teaching me about French cooking. She always had my place set at the opposite end of the table from hers, very formal and uncomfortable, and she was explaining the chocolate mousse we were having for dessert. I didn't want to tell her that I already knew what a mousse was and that Madame Sosostris could make an even better one than Rose. I know I have a tendency to come on like a smarty-pants kid, and Aunt Lucy did seem to be enjoying herself, explaining about how it was really just a fluffy chocolate pudding, when all of a sudden she let out a squeak and her eyes got that glass look.

I peered under the table, and there was Sam, who had just lain down with his head over Aunt Lucy's foot. I think it's nice when a dog loves you enough to lay his head across your foot, but I knew that Aunt Lucy didn't share my opinion, so I hauled Sam off to my bedroom. I was hoping she'd go on describing the chocolate mousse, but she'd tightened up by the time I got back. And she was sneezing, too . . . Honestly, I never did believe those sneezes.

I never saw the worst moments. The one Rose enjoyed most—but Aunt Lucy sure didn't—was when she'd left her bedroom door ajar and woken up one morning to find Sam's head asleep beside her on the pillow. She'd screamed, "Sam!"—and he'd said, "Woof," and gone back to his box.

Then there was the incident of Mr. Watkins. Rose told me she happened to have some work in the hall, so she couldn't help but overhear them talking in the living room. About my "schooling" and whether I was "adjusting" or not. I think it was the very day that I was "adjusting" my bookcases up to the apartment. Well, I don't think it came to actual biting—I hope not anyway—but it seems that Sam, who had not adjusted to Mr. Watkins too well, chased him up on a chair, and it took all of Rose's persuasion and strength to drag Sam back into my bedroom.

Then came the big blowup. It happened on the great day . . . You never know in the morning what you'll find in the night.

I was sitting in the kitchen, having breakfast. Rose was keeping me company with a cup of coffee and doing the *New York Times* crossword puzzle, which she said meant just as much to her as her first cup of coffee. Maurice was there, too, fidgeting and waiting for Aunt Lucy.

Suddenly there came this terrific crashing from Aunt Lucy's bedroom. We all froze. Then we heard Aunt Lucy squeaking, "Oh! oh! oh!"—and we rushed to see what had happened.

Aunt Lucy was standing on the threshold to her bathroom—I guess she'd been in there doing a last little bit of primping—and staring at the catastrophe. The catastrophe was Sam, lying under the wreckage of her vanity table, covered with a gooey mixture of perfume and face powder. He'd obviously been up on his hind legs, enjoying a sniff, and pulled the whole thing over on him. Half the bottles were broken, and all of them were leaking, and he was some smelly mess! (But despite it all, he was still grinning.)

I heard Rose murmur, "Oh, man, that dog has really done it now!" Then she pitched in and started to clean things up.

I was going to begin to apologize for Sam, when Aunt Lucy said, as loftily as a little woman could, "Timothy, I want that mongrel out of here." I thought she meant, just out of her bedroom. "Lock him in your bathroom. Then come into the living room. It's time we had a talk." She was being as formal and grownup as possible, but a fit of sneezing got hold of her and sort of undid the act. I still think it was only all the perfume in the air.

I stowed Sam in the bathtub and told him to stay there—

by now he had his tail between his legs—and went in to face the music. Aunt Lucy was calmer and talked very reasonably. Which made me even more worried. "Timmy," she said, "I'm afraid that you'll have to get rid of Sam."

"Get rid of—"

"Yes, dear." She forced out a laugh. "I'm sorry, the simple truth is that I'm allergic to him."

"Aunt Lucy, that's just the—"

"Whatever it is, dear," she interrupted, "I've made up my mind." It didn't help for me to notice that Maurice was out in the hall eavesdropping. I wouldn't have minded if it had been Rose I was being put down in front of. "Sam's a part of your life that's behind you," Aunt Lucy went on. "I haven't wanted to say anything, because I've wanted you to—" Even Aunt Lucy couldn't stomach that word "adjust." "I've wanted you to feel at home here, but those things you've brought into your bedroom, bones and that awful little idol—oh, yes, I admit I've been snooping—I think they're downright morbid. I don't mind your changing the things that I picked out, but—"

"I didn't know you picked everything out, Aunt Lucy. If I had, I'd have left it the way it was."

"That's very sweet, Timmy, but—"

But—I'm not going to go over the whole of the talk we had. It still squeezes my stomach to think about it. What it came down to was, I had to get rid of Sam *that day*! Aunt

Lucy tried to sweeten the sour by saying I could pick out a nice new poodle puppy if I wanted another dog. I tried to imagine Sam with his tail and paws cut into poodle puff balls, but it wasn't possible—much less funny. There was also some stuff about my not having made any friends in Sutton Place. Which I had—Rose—but I shut up and let her talk.

The talk ended with Aunt Lucy not wanting to look at me—"Shall I take care of it, dear?" she said, and "No, thank you," I answered—and me not wanting to look at her. Maurice drove her off to a committee meeting somewhere. Aunt Lucy was very big on committees then.

The only thing I could think of to do—because I couldn't think of anything—was to get Sam washed. I managed to stretch out the bath for an hour. He was covered with eight kinds of smells, so it wasn't too hard. Sam's always seemed to like baths, too, unlike most dogs. Meanwhile, though, as I scrubbed him down and he lifted his forelegs one after the other so I could get him really clean, I was formulating my first plan . . . I had to plan a lot, last spring.

But before I took him into the kitchen, I stowed away all my stuff in the closet. If Aunt Lucy didn't like my bones and pipes and things, I thought it was best to get them out of her sight.

By now it was getting toward eleven o'clock. Rose was futzing around the sink, just making up work to do, when Sam and I came in. She knew the crunch was on.

"Rose," I began, "I want to thank you for cleaning up Aunt Lucy's room. It won't happen again."

"I guess it won't." Rose was always one for getting things out in the open where you could look at them honestly. "Your aunt told me she was asking you to get him out of the house."

"I'm glad you happened to bring that up, Rose," I said, "because I wanted to ask you something. Do you like Sam?"

"Sure I like him, Tim—"

"That's good!" I pressed in fast. "Because I'm giving him to you! For a present. And, also, I thought I might come into your room to visit him now and then."

For a while Rose didn't say anything. Her face was working, to decide what to say. Then she made up her mind. "Timmy, that is certainly the richest present I've ever been offered, because I know how much Sam means to you. But Miss Farr wants him out of the apartment. I can't keep him with me, as much as I'd dearly love to." I'd known all along, of course. It was just a wild hope. But wild hopes sometimes pay off. (The wildest one I ever had came later that day.) Rose went on, "Would you like me to ask my friends, if anybody—"

"Oh, no. No, thank you, Rose." I couldn't stand the idea of Sam living with strangers, and maybe so far away that I couldn't go visit him. "I'll work it out."

In the sticky silence that followed, Maurice came back. It was part of his deal with Aunt Lucy that he got lunch—a big hot lunch, even in summer, he made sure of that—every day.

"Modom says she won't be home until evening. She's been made chairman of the Friends of Retired Librarians Committee. It's a very great honor." He toed Sam disdainfully away from under the table so he could sit down, and his eyes picked me over with a smile. "However, she said that I was to be at the disposal of young Master Farr all afternoon. For anything he might wish."

"I don't wish anything!" I snapped. "I can do what I have to myself."

Rose put some space between us by saying, "Hey, Tim, I'm cooking Maurice a cube steak—you want one, too?"

"No, thank you, Rose," I said. "I'm going down to Greenwich Village. In a taxi!" Aunt Lucy was making me give my dog away, but she always made sure I had plenty of pocket money.

I went into my bedroom and put on my jacket. When I got back to the kitchen, Maurice's *hot* cube steak was cooking, and Rose was nervously doing her crossword puzzle.

"Say goodbye to Rose, Sam," I said. He put his paws up in her lap and licked one hand.

" 'Bye, Sam," said Rose and squinted down into her puzzle. "Now will someone please explain to me just what's an eleven-letter word meaning 'to dispose of completely'?"

Maurice had the answer: "EXTERMINATE!"

4

The Great Day

"What mortal or immortal being craves admittance to—"

"It's just me, Madame Sosostris," I called from the front room. She always goes into her spiel when the bell over the front door goes off.

"Hi, Tim!" She came out from the back with her usual clothes on: Levi's, a purple blouse, and the tie-dyed turban. She bent over and hugged and kissed me. "It's always a whiff of ectoplasm to see you, lad!"

"How's business?" I was kind of afraid to start the subject.

"Oh, the junk keeps moving all right. But nothing exciting. Had the Willy sisters in yesterday. And read a palm this morning."

"Anything interesting in it?"

"Nah! Might just as well have been the yellow pages. You can't imagine how *dull* some lives are! How's by you, Tim?"

"I have worries, Madame Sosostris."

"I was wondering about that." She nodded. "Your face looks like something left over from a raid by a poltergeist. Come on in the kitchen—we'll thrash it out over a cuppa tea."

I told her all about it. And just as I was getting down to the nitty-gritty, there came the *second* horrendous crash that day. Sam, of course. He always enjoyed browsing as much as I, or Lorenzo or Madame Sosostris, but he didn't do it as carefully. It was an old Egyptian tray this time, made of bronze, so fortunately it didn't break. But there was this big ugly dent in one corner.

"Don't give it a thought!" said Madame Sosostris. She waved her hand grandly in the air. "Nobody'll know if that dent was made today or two hundred years ago. It adds to the antiquity. I'll jack up the price ten bucks!"

I love Madame S. But my heart felt like a wrung-out dishrag. "It won't work," I said.

I hadn't even asked her yet, but Madame Sosostris grabbed me by the shoulders and shouted, "Of course Sam can live down here! I know how much that dog means to you—so he means that much to me."

"He'd wreck the place. All the glass—"

"The hell with the glass! I'll get rid of the glass. I'll specialize in metal junk. Besides, when I have my breakthrough as a medium, I'm going to give it all up anyway. Sam can't damage the Spirits!"

"Madame Sosostris—it just won't work."

She knew it wouldn't, too. "Back to the kitchen. I got a crystal ball last week from the Gypsies' Association of Spain. It turned out to be a dud, but don't give up hope."

"Oh, Madame Sosostris, this is serious! We can't use a silly thing like a crystal—" The way to the kitchen led through the séance room, and on the way back I suddenly felt Lorenzo's books all around. It was just as if the whole library had whispered something softly to me. I had been planning to smuggle them up a few at a time to Sutton Place, but "Now," they seemed to be saying, "*now!*"

"Madame Sosostris," I said, "you remember Lorenzo's will? His books? He said there were wonders in them—and unexpected assistance—"

"I remember—"

"Come on. We've got to look through every one!"

A frantic search began. It took us practically all afternoon. And we did come up with some fascinating stuff before I discovered the spell.

Madame Sosostris found the formula for a love potion and suggested we cook it up and give it to Aunt Lucy, so then she'd love Sam. But it sounded too icky and dangerous to me.

She also turned up a curse Lorenzo had heard from a Tanganyikan witch doctor on his travels in Africa. " 'May baboons bathe in your blighted blood!' Boy, that would certainly freeze the landlord!"

"Madame Sosostris, I don't want to curse anybody," I said. "Please keep looking for something constructive."

I was going through the section of books that made up Lorenzo's diary when I found it.

"Here's something. Listen, Madame Sosostris. 'London, May 14, 1938. Arrived this morning and went immediately to the British Museum, Near Eastern Division. Could not locate the manuscript I desired—a treatise on certain psychogenic herbs by the court physician of Haroun Al-Raschid—but did discover most interesting translation, purportedly made by a Dominican friar in 1601, of Al-Hazred's *Necronomicon*. Contains much esoteric information. Especially fascinated by following spell, a verse for conjuring the Slave of the Carpet—whoever that might be. Upon trial, however, it proved a failure. Perhaps spoken in the original Arabic, its success might be greater.' And here's the spell, Madame Sosostris—

Genie formed of earth and sky,
Skin of night, with lunar eye,
Bone of mountain, blood of sea—
Come hither, Thou, and wait on me!"

Nothing happened.

"Lorenzo was right," said Madame Sosostris. "It's as much of a fake as the Gypsies' Association of Spain."

Nothing happened, I mean, outside my head. But *inside* —it was as if a quick wind blew through my brain.

"Where can I find someone who knows Arabic?"

"Oh, Tim, come on! You don't believe that nonsense. It's my crystal ball all over again."

"Madame Sosostris!—you *know* how important Lorenzo always said language was. And particularly in spells. Now *where?*"

"Well, at the library. Or the National Museum. They've got a big Near Eastern wing up there. But—"

"Can I take this page out of the diary? With just the spell on it?"

"They're your books, Tim."

"Come on, Sam!" I shouted. "Goodbye, Madame S.! Don't sell the glass!"

The National Museum has always been one of my favorite places. I caught Lorenzo's enthusiasm the first time we went there. I love a spot, like the National or Madame Sosostris's antique shop, where the things of the past that might have died still have a chance.

There are bushes in front of the building, and I told Sam to get in under the leaves and stay there—and stay away from other dogs, too, because this was a very important day. There was no time for socializing. Then I ran up the big flight of stairs to the entrance. Usually I like to march up solemnly—it feels formal and fun—but not today.

I asked a guard where I could find an expert in Arabic, of course without telling him why—no sense wasting time with disbelief. He said the chairman's office of the Near Eastern Division was just down that hall and pointed the way.

But the chairman, when I told him I wanted a spell translated, looked busy and said, "Try Mr. Dickinson. Basement rear, to the left. He's an expert on spells."

It turned out that Mr. Dickinson wasn't an expert on spells—as yet—although he did know Arabic very well. His field was Near Eastern crockery. I found him in this crazy little room all full of pieces of broken pots and bowls. A lot of them came from a time much earlier than I was after, but they were interesting anyway. It was his job to try to fit the pieces together. I liked him for the patience it must have taken. And I also liked the way his hair, which was fluffy and white, puffed out around his ears.

"Sir," I began at the door, "I have this spell that I'd like translated into Arabic."

"Oh, how delightful! A spell." Naturally he didn't believe it either. "Come in, come in. But I'm afraid that someone's been teasing you. My study is crockery."

"Oh, that's all right," I said. "Would you just translate this, please?"

I gave him the page from Lorenzo's diary, and he read the verse over, murmuring, "Charming! Absolutely charming!"

"I'm sorry to bother you," I said. "But I don't speak Arabic. Just English. And a little bit of Latin."

"I tell you what," said Mr. Dickinson. "I'll write this out phonetically. You just have to pronounce the syllables."

"That will be fine," I said.

He kind of mumbled and hummed to himself as he worked. Then when he was finished, he said, "Now I'll just read it once aloud to—"

"*No!* Please." I took the paper out of his hand. "I'll do that."

"A very curious incantation," said Mr. Dickinson. "Might I ask who invented it?"

"A man named Al-Hazred."

Beneath his puff balls Mr. Dickinson's ears pricked up. "Akbar Al-Hazred? The Master of Magic?"

That wind began to blow through my brain again. Just a little breeze now—but growing. "You know him?"

"Akbar Al-Rizna Al-Hazred—" Mr. Dickinson's voice got kind of teachy, but I didn't mind—"the Master of Magic, as subsequent sorcerers, warlocks, and alchemists styled him, was a man who lived in the eighth century of our era. And he was reputed to be a great and powerful wizard. Upstairs we have a tapestry—the Wizard's Tapestry, it's called—supposed to have been woven by him, or at least under his command. In fact, we have *two* rooms upstairs containing objects that are supposed to have belonged to him."

I'd been in one of them, with Lorenzo. The wind started up in my heart now—strong. "This is a spell to summon the Slave of the Carpet—how strange. The Slave of the Carpet." Mr. Dickinson puckered his forehead at me and was quiet awhile.

I got my voice back into my throat and said, "What's strange about it, sir?"

"Well—everyone has always supposed that this—fabric, shall we say?—was a tapestry. It's so absolutely gorgeous! But it's barely possible that it might have been a carpet. The coincidence is that in the thing there's woven the figure of— a genie."

At that moment I knew. The wind blowing through me had only been hope. But now I was sure. After all, it stood to reason that if the spell was going to work anywhere, it surely would right in front of the carpet. Mr. Dickinson called it "coincidence." Some people say "fate" or "luck" or "chance." But there are times when everything fits together, like one of Mr. Dickinson's broken pots. I *knew*. And I was petrified! Because anyone who fools around with the Occult Sciences is asking for trouble. There are lots of things that ought to be kept out. But there was no help for it—I had to go on. And it had to be today.

"Thank you, Mr. Dickinson." I stood up, and my legs felt as shaky as my voice. "I think I'll just have a look at that tapestry."

"Yes, I daresay you will." I was out the door and heading for the staircase when he called, "Now don't be too disappointed if—" But I had already stopped hearing him.

I know the National pretty well, and I was making a beeline for the Near Eastern wing when this bell went off. I didn't even know I'd heard it until a guard grabbed me by the arm and said, "Closing time, young man."

"Sir," I tried to explain, "I have to see the Wizard's—"

"My boy—" he began propelling me back where I'd come from—"when the National closes, it closes for everyone!"

"Yes, sir." I gave up—hope, too, almost—and went back through the Renaissance rooms toward the entrance.

But then I came to the Fourteenth-Century Florence room. It was empty. The guards had cleared everybody out. I saw this big wooden chest, with carvings all over it. And right away I said to myself, If the lid lifts—yes! If it's locked, then no . . . I'm not usually superstitious, but I sure was that day.

The lid lifted. I went in like an eel, lowered the lid over me, and began my wait. In the dark.

5

Abdullah

I was scared three ways, the hours I lay in that chest. First,
because of what I knew I was going to have to do; second,
I thought a guard might find me and think I was one of
those creeps who steal paintings from museums; and third,
I was afraid for Sam. I could imagine him padding out
from the bushes and looking up the stairs for me. But I
trusted Sam. He always usually does what he's told.

For the first few hours I could hear the charwomen

sloshing and slopping around on the floor. I only hoped that nobody thought to clean inside an antique. And they didn't.

Then there came an itchy time when I was dying to lift the lid and look out, but didn't dare. A good thing, too. The guards were making their rounds, and every half hour or so I'd hear a man's step going *klomp klomp klomp* through the Renaissance rooms—much harder than the sloshing of the charwomen.

But then came the worst time of all: a dead silence. I still didn't dare to lift the lid. I had to, though—I was getting buggy.

Through the crack I could see that there was a little weak light drifting in from somewhere into the room outside. The room was empty. I guess the lid didn't really creak like breaking wood as I squeaked my way out, but it sounded that way to me.

The most important thing, at this point, was that I didn't want to be alone. I went downstairs to the first floor—the Renaissance rooms are on the second—then traced my way down to the basement. I heard a guard adjusting his chair beside the main entrance, but I didn't see him and he didn't see me. There were little stand-up lights left on here and there, so I could see my way. I judged about where I was and began to look for a window. The one I found was pretty high up, and I had to drag a chair over—very quietly!—to reach it. I was praying it would have an inside lock, and it did. But the bolt was huge, and every tug sounded just like a thunderbolt.

I got it open at last and lifted the window. Then I whistled softly and called, "Sam—"

In a minute I heard him sniffling and shuffling, and there he was! I was so glad to see him that I kissed him and stroked his head even before I lifted him in. Then came another crisis, because he's so heavy I was certain I'd drop him.

But I landed him all right. "Now be quiet, Sam. And *really* be quiet!" I ordered. "This is serious."

We made our way upstairs, Sam padding close behind me. It was easy to avoid the guards who were still awake, because now that the museum was empty, they were laughing and cracking jokes and talking very loud to each other. But it sounded as if there were two of them up in the Renaissance rooms, so we took the back staircase.

Which meant that we had to go through the Egyptian wing. I wasn't too happy about that. There's this enormous statue of the god Thoth—the God of Wisdom and Magic— the one with a falcon's head on top of a human body. His stone eyes seemed to be looking at us. They followed us all the way across the room.

We went past a seated Buddha in the staircase, too. I couldn't figure out his smile. It might have been encouragement—it might have been some secret that he knew of in advance. He wasn't telling, though.

There was no secret about the frowning bronze Roman gladiator at the top of the stairs. He was telling me to turn back.

But I didn't . . . I went into the Al-Hazred rooms.

There was one of those little stand-up lights the guards put around in the first room. But none in the second. I could barely make out the tapestry. But what I saw was enough to make me wish I'd never even found that spell.

There was a genie up there on the wall, all right, inside the tapestry, and framed by this very elaborate border of curlicuing leaves and flowers. But what a genie! I was expecting some Hollywood type, with a smirk on his face and his arms crossed over a big bare chest. But this genie was fully clothed, from the turban on his head, with a red jewel in the center, right down through a white blouse and black pantaloons, to gray slippers on his feet. He was standing in front of a desert landscape woven into the tapestry. Very barren and awful—just sand and sand and sand. In the sky were a couple of stars, with a very thin crescent moon, like a little silver grin in the night. But the awful thing was his attitude. His arms were raised, as if he were lunging right out of the fabric, and his face was all twisted in a terrible rage. If ever I saw fury and hatred, I saw it in that tapestry.

And those eyes!—just burning out at me, as if they were already alive. It's a wonder his eyes didn't set the whole thing on fire.

Even Sam panicked. He took one look, and his tail slumped down between his legs, and he slunk away off in a corner, behind a big urn.

I was all alone in front of the tapestry, carpet, whatever it was. I took out the spell, and by the little light I read it.

I'm not going to put down the Arabic. I'm pretty sure it's safe now. But I'm not going to put it down anyway.

For a second there was nothing. And I have to admit I was almost relieved. I don't honestly know what I was expecting. Thunder, maybe. And lightning. But it wasn't like that at all. Looking up at those eyes, I suddenly realized they *were* alive. It would have been a big relief if there *had* been thunder. The genie figure from the tapestry was just there, all at once, in front of me, with his arms still lifted above his head and that awful expression on his face . . . And big!—was he big—about six foot six, as big as in the tapestry.

I thought to myself, If he clobbers me with one of those hands—

But he didn't. In one single movement—a very beautiful, graceful movement—he brought his hands together, the right over the left, glided down on his knees, with his hands outstretched till they touched the floor, then touched the floor with his forehead as well. And then he whispered something in Arabic.

"Sir," I gulped. "I don't know that much Arabic. Do you speak any English?"

With his head still lowered, he said, "Master, I speak all the tongues of Earth, the Dark World, and Glorious Paradise." Then, very slowly, he lifted his face, and for the first time I saw that secret smile of his. "What I said was, 'Lord, I come from endless servitude to do your bidding.' "

"You mean you're not going to hit me—?"

"I would plunge my fist in the fire that knows no quenching first."

"And—and you'll help me?"

"Master, to satisfy your will was I created."

"—And do what I ask?"

"Were it even to steal the seven precious eggs of the Giant Roc that nests on the summit of Jabal Aja!"

"Sam!" I forgot where we were and shouted, "Sam! You can come out. He's safe!"

Sam came tearing from behind the urn, put his paws up on the Genie's shoulders, and started to lick his cheek. I thought that was going a little far, and it might make him angry. It didn't, though. His smile got even longer, and he put his arm around Sam and let him go right on licking his face. Sam caught even more of my excitement and began to bark like mad.

"Shh, Sam!" I remembered. "You'll wake the guards!" Sam whimpered a little, because he was enjoying his barking, but then he shut up.

And me—I was just bug-eyed! "Um—do you have a name? My name is Timothy Farr."

"Yes, Master Timothy. But may I rise first?"

"Oh, gosh, yes! Please! I didn't know—" You get flustered when you realize a genie is waiting for your orders.

He stood up, towering over me and Sam and everything else in the room. "The Wizard, Al-Hazred, who made me, called me Abdullah."

"Did he really make you—?"

"Yes, master." What a wonderful voice he had, too! As rich and deep and dark as his skin. "Over a thousand years ago he kneaded my flesh from the golden sand of the burning desert, mixed with the darkness of starless night. From the running salt tides of the sea he drew my blood, and carved my bones from granite mountains. Moonlight he filtered for my eyes, and he tore my voice from the throat of the roaring simoom. Upon my finger he placed the Ring of Immortality." Abdullah held out his left hand. On the longest finger a beautiful silver ring softly glowed in the dark. (I never did find out whether it was silver or platinum or some magical metal.) "And when he had made me, he said to me—'*Live!*' And I lived. I stood up and I laughed—I *laughed!*—because I was alive." A big boom of laughter began in his chest.

"Shh, shh! Please," I warned.

"Pardon, master. But to laugh is bliss, after all the centuries when my soul was imprisoned amid the threads." He turned to look at the tapestry. His figure was still there, but different now—just a little bit changed. The eyes looked as if they *were* woven now, not real eyes, trapped. "Oh, the fury I felt when I knew my fate! I believe I would have destroyed the Master of Magic himself."

"I could see. But why did the Wizard lock you up in the rug?"

"I offended him, master. I fell in love—with one of the women from Al-Hazred's harem. A mortal failing in one created to be immortal. As punishment the Wizard confined me to the frightful carpet."

"But I let you out—"

"You did, my master." Abdullah could bring his hands together in an obeisance and bow his head, and still be dignified and noble. "May your beard be blessed!" He could also glance up with that smile and add, "When you have a beard. What service may I perform for you?"

"As a matter of fact," I explained, "I do have a little problem. Sam."

The Genie stroked Sam's head. There was a chuckle riding inside his voice. "I take it that this is Sam."

"Yes. He's my dog, Sam. My Aunt Lucy wants me to get rid of him."

Abdullah stroked his chin with his thumb and forefinger, and then matter-of-factly announced, "I will turn Aunt Lucy into a fly and summon a toad from the nearest garden to appear and eat the fly."

"Oh, for gosh sake," I said, "don't do that! She's my father's only sister. And she means well—only she doesn't know how. But I don't want to have to get rid of Sam."

Abdullah paced up and down. I could see he was thinking of different solutions. Finally he stopped and said, "Oh, master, this is difficult. If it were only to move a mountain or build a palace, I could perform the task as easily as the dove constructs her simple nest. But how can Sam both go and stay?" He brooded a minute more. "I must observe the situation. Let me come to you again."

I got a bit nervous at hearing that, after being so sure at first. Maybe this Genie wouldn't work out after all. "Can you find your way around New York? I live way over in Sutton Place—"

"New York, master—?"

"The city where we are. Look—" There was a window in the Al-Hazred room, but the shade was drawn. I lifted it for him a crack. Far off you could see the buildings of Central Park South, and beyond that the Empire State Building. I love New York when it's lit up at night.

"Oh, master," Abdullah murmured. " 'Tis bigger even than Baghdad and the pinnacled cities of the Farthest East. But yes, my little master Timothy, give me a single night— to prowl and explore—and I shall be able to find my way— even in this most magnificent of cities."

"Well—all right then. If you're sure." I gave him the

address. "Now, can you get us out of here without waking anyone up?"

"Come, master. And Sam." Abdullah put his hand on my shoulder and steered me out of the tapestry room. What a whopping hand, too! I don't know if it was that he was so big, or the genie magic in it, but I felt my shoulder tingling.

We didn't meet any guards till we got to the front door of the museum. One was tipped back in his chair, asleep, against the latch. I think he heard us in his sleep, because he began to mumble something and his hands made little jerky motions; but Abdullah just rested his fingertips on the guard's forehead and whispered softly, "Peace, mortal. And dream of thy delight."

That really turned me on! I mean, somebody else would have said only, "Stay asleep," or "Conk out, man." But not Abdullah. I love a person who knows his words, and, believe me, there's *nobody* who knows how to talk the way a genie does.

"I guess they locked the door—" I began.

But Abdullah reached out his hand toward the lock and kind of chanted, "Thou mighty bolts—apart! I know thy tightened secret art." I got another look at that genie smile of his as the bolts slowly separated and the door swung open.

Oh, boy, I remember it still . . . At this point you can

imagine where my head—and my heart, too—was at. A
place where the impossible turns real . . .

When we got to the bottom of the stairs, Sam and I both
looked back. There he stood: Abdullah—my Genie—sil-
houetted in the dim light from the museum behind him.

The second most exciting day in my life . . .

But it ended badly, drearily predictable—after all that
magic, too.

I was hoping against hope that Aunt Lucy would be
asleep. But as soon as the cab pulled up in front of the
apartment house, the doorman rushed out and said,
"Timothy Farr, where *have* you been? Your aunt's half
crazy—"

It was one o'clock in the morning, and from a grownup's
point of view, for a kid my age that's a very bad time to be
still at large.

"Timothy—!"

The whole apartment was bubbling with worry. Rose
was still up, and Mr. Watkins was also there.

"I'm sorry, Aunt Lucy." I really *was* sorry, too. If it
wasn't something critical, like conjuring a Genie, I'd never
have dreamed of staying out all hours.

"I've even called the police—!"

"I'd better attend to that."

While Mr. Watkins attended on the telephone, Aunt

Lucy went on dressing me down. "I'm really more pro-
voked than I can say." She had a right to be, too. I'm all
in favor of Women's Lib, and that includes the liberty to
be furious. But with Aunt Lucy being so short, it just
didn't work. She wanted to seem in a towering rage, but
with her it was only a jiggling rage.

To make matters worse, right then Sam plodded in from
the hall, and as he always did in the presence of Aunt
Lucy, he sat down dreamily in front of her and leaned his
head against her leg. "Sam!" I don't think she would have
kicked him, but I dragged him off right away anyway.
"Now this *is* the last straw! I promised myself—when
the boy comes back, I won't be too angry, because I realize
that you've had to—but you haven't."

"Aunt Lucy, don't worry," I said—sort of begged. "The
problem of Sam can be solved."

"I know that." She withdrew into dignity. "I shall solve
it myself."

"Miss Farr—" Rose interrupted, to give us some air
—"I'd like to ask—have you had any supper, Tim?"

"I'm honestly not hungry—"

"Make him a sandwich, Rose, if you would." Aunt Lucy
took Rose's way out of all the quarreling. "We'll discuss
this tomorrow."

In the kitchen, while she was making a spiced ham and
lettuce sandwich, with mayonnaise, which she knew was

my favorite, even Rose wouldn't talk to me. There are some people whose silences are worse than other people's noise.

I tried to start a conversation. "She's awfully angry, isn't she?"

"Man, you've gone and done it now" was all that Rose would say to me.

I put Sam in his box at the foot of my bed, kissed him good night, and said, "Boy, we are *both* in the doghouse now! That Genie Abdullah had better pan out." He'd already begun to feel like a dream.

The last thing I did that night was to hide the Arabic genie spell. I thought about it a very long time and decided the safest place would be way back in the top of my closet, behind all my things. My Good-Luck Devil is hollow—the eyes are the openings—and I carefully folded the paper up and pushed it in through the left one.

6

Dooley

I slept late the next morning . . . Too late.

Usually the first thing I do when I wake up is crawl down the bed, say good morning to Sam in his box, and pet him awhile. Then I give him his breakfast, two biscuits from the can I keep under the bed. But on that morning Sam was not there. And Sam has this habit—I think it's half love and half habit—of *never* getting up until I do.

I dressed as fast as possible, stamping out as many of

the fears that kept cropping up as I could and went into the kitchen. Aunt Lucy was there talking to Rose. I heard her saying, "It's very unlike Maurice. He's been so reliable all these years. Oh, good morning, Timothy. You certainly slept—"

"Good morning, Aunt Lucy, good morning, Rose, where's Sam?" I said.

Rose turned around to look at a counter with a bowl on it and said to me, not wanting to see me, "Well, hi there, Rip Van Winkle! Look, I just happen to have this batter. You want pancakes for breakfast?"

Honestly!—the way the minds of some people work! I'm surprised Rose let Aunt Lucy put her up to it. If ever I heard a bribe, or a consolation prize, or condolences, it was those pancakes. "No, thank you. I'm not really all that hungry," I said. "Please, Aunt Lucy—where *is* Sam?"

"Oh, Timothy—" her voice sounded like a violin string, tuned too high—"this is such a topsy-turvy morning. I've just had a call from the agency, about Maurice—"

"I don't give a *damn* about Maurice—"

"Timothy!" She got out of her embarrassment by being indignant. "I will not tolerate language like that from—" And gave me the whole lecture.

I did feel like swearing, too. And I could have, very well. When Lorenzo or Madame Sosostris got really mad at somebody, they'd let go a string that made quite an impression—on me, too. But I bit my tongue and said only, "I'd just like to know—where my *dog* is."

"Timothy, you didn't seem to know how to—dispose of—" That high voice of hers got stuck in her throat.

"Aunt Lucy—did you give Sam *away*? To strangers—?"

"I have taken care of the matter. Let that be—"

"Where *is* he?"

"Young man, do not raise your voice to me!"

We were heading into a battle royal, with swearing and a lot of other things, too, as far as I was concerned, when the buzzer at the servants' entrance rang.

"Saved by the bell," Rose muttered on her way to the door.

I was going to ask her nicely, one last time, where Sam was, before I started to punch out Aunt Lucy, when I saw who was standing in the kitchen door.

It was him! Abdullah! All dressed up in a uniform like Maurice's. But instead of that usual sly smile, he had a big grin on, at my amazement.

"Are you the man from Maurice's agency?" asked Aunt Lucy.

"Yes, mistress," said Abdullah. I couldn't be sure, but I thought he winked at me.

"Now, am I to understand that Maurice just—"

"—vanished!" said Abdullah. His smile got back to the secret it always seemed to know.

"Well, I think it's all very mysterious," dithered Aunt Lucy. "People don't just—vanish."

"I assure you, mistress," said Abdullah authoritatively, "that that is just what Maurice has done."

"Strange," murmured Aunt Lucy.

"Mmm," Abdullah echoed her with a rumble from his chest. "There's a lot of strangeness around these days."

"And I take it that you would like Maurice's position?"

"Yes, mistress."

"Well—I suppose, for a week or so, we might try it. But if Maurice comes back—"

"Mistress, Maurice is *not* coming back."

"I trust that you have references," said Aunt Lucy in a dry employer-type voice.

"Oh, certainly, mistress." Abdullah put his hand in his inside jacket pocket—I'm sure I heard his fingers click—and brought out a bunch of letters. And I *know* they weren't there, until he got them in by magic.

Aunt Lucy glanced at the letters, pretending to be me-thodical, and finally did recognize a couple of names. "Oh, yes—the Cornelius Vintons and Mrs. Callisher Davidson. I'm sure you'll do very well."

"Thank you, mistress." Abdullah bowed slightly. But his grin didn't put her down.

"Now I'd like you to meet my nephew—Timothy Farr."

"Little Master Timothy—" I got a little bow myself and

a look like a private laugh that went straight through my eyes to my brain. I'd been standing there all this time like a gawk, believing and not believing, both.

"And this is Rose Jackson."

I know I keep harping on his smile—but a smile is where you can tell a lot—and his did something else now, as Abdullah made his courtly bow to Rose. "Mistress."

Rose was wary—the way women are, at first. "Pleased to meet you—"

But Abdullah continued to be gallant. "And I you—Rose."

"Now your name is—?"

"Abdullah, mistress."

"Abdullah—" Aunt Lucy mouthed the word over. "Such an interesting name. Has it been in your family long?"

"For over a thousand years, mistress."

"Really! My goodness." Aunt Lucy didn't know what to make of that, but she made whatever she could of it, and then said, "But we can't really call you Abdullah. I tell you what—we'll just call you Dooley—is that all right with you?"

"Perfectly, mistress."

So it was Aunt Lucy who named him. An inspiration. I think her change began right there. And I hate to admit it, but I think that that was the first time I really liked Aunt Lucy. Despite what she had just done to Sam.

"Well—that's settled." She remembered how bad the

scene had been before Dooley showed up. Her eyes glanced at me once, then flew away like frightened birds. "Uh—have you had breakfast this morning, Dooley?"

"No, mistress."

"Then I suggest that you and Timothy have breakfast together. And I'm sure Rose will join you for a cup of coffee." She was beating a retreat to the hall. "I have to do my desk today. Pay bills and things like that. You three get acquainted—and—and—" she stopped in the door— "and, Dooley, you don't really have to call me mistress. I've always been terribly liberal." She made good her escape.

"Rose," I said quietly but quaking inside, "where is he?"

"Now look, mister, I will not become—"

"Rose—are you my friend?"

"—involved in an argument between you and—"

"Rose—*are* you my friend?"

She sighed, gave up, and said flatly, "The Houston Street dog pound. One sixty-eight West Houston Street." She had it all memorized to tell me . . . I love Rose.

But I didn't think of that then. "The *dog* pound!" I shouted. "That means they're going to kill him! Dooley— come on!"

In the elevator down to the garage—I was urging it under my breath to hurry—another fear grabbed me. "Dooley —can you drive?"

"Oh, master," he said scornfully, "I have driven the Wizard's Chariot of Winds."

"That's fine, but my aunt owns a Cadillac."

"It will hold no mystery for me."

Maybe not, but the first thing he did when we got the keys from the attendant—that's how safe Aunt Lucy's building is, you can leave your keys in the garage—was to put us in reverse and wham us into the wall. Dooley got a grim expression and gripped the wheel determinedly. "Fear not, little master." Then he said to the car, "Machine— proceed!"

And that Cadillac purred out in the street just as sweetly as you could ask. I'm sure it was running on magic, because Dooley never bothered to shift gears or brake. It just did what he willed it to.

I was jouncing around on the front seat beside him, wondering if we'd make it in time, when about two blocks down Second Avenue he brought up something completely irrelevant. "Master," he calmly asked, just as if we weren't in a race for Sam's life, "discuss Rose Jackson."

"She's a girl who's a singer and who's working for Aunt Lucy to pay for her lessons. Hey, Dooley!—that was a red light—"

"Very pretty."

"No, when it's red you have to stop. On the *green* lights you go."

"Then let them all be green." He snapped his right hand, as if he were flicking water—but it was magic—off his fingertips. Every light on Second Avenue turned green!

I was sitting there, swimming in the wonder of that, when we came to the cop. "His hand is up now, Dooley."

"A greeting, no doubt."

I realized I was going to have to give this Genie driving lessons. (Later I found out that he'd been so busy exploring about me last night that he hadn't bothered with simple things.) "No, when a cop's hand is up, you have to stop. You go forward when he beckons—like this."

He did it with just one finger this time, crooking it forward. And I never will forget that cop's face when he wanted us to stop, and his hand just kept rising in front of him, beckoning us on . . . I really would have enjoyed that ride, if it hadn't been for Sam.

Behind Sam there was also another nag—not nearly as important, of course. "Dooley, you didn't do anything like —evaporate Maurice, did you? I didn't much like him, but—"

"Master, at this very moment Maurice dwells in his own dull vision of Paradise. In my comings and goings last night, and my picking over of many minds that appertain to you, I learned that Maurice had only one dream: to retire to a city named St. Petersburg, in a state called, I believe, Florida. Thus, this morning Mister Maurice woke up in the Golden Age Motel, 136 Palm Drive, St. Petersburg, Florida. And he found, beside his bed, a bank book containing not only his own hoarded savings, but enough in addition to keep him in his middling bliss for the rest of his days."

The way he could just take care of people!—as if he were dealing cards. "But Dooley," I said, "won't Maurice be a little suspicious—if he goes to sleep in New York and wakes up in Florida?"

"Little Master Timothy, in my dealings with men I have found that they fall in two groups. There are some— and I believe you are one such yourself—who seek out the forces that shape their fate. As for the others—when Mister Maurice sees the amount of money that has been deposited in his name in the First National Bank of St. Petersburg, Florida, he will be well content to live in ignorance."

"If you say so, Dooley." As long as I didn't have to feel guilty about the evaporation of Maurice, I wasn't going to worry about it.

Besides, we'd reached Houston Street. And there was the dog pound, in all its ugliness. A terrible place, like a concentration camp, with horrible concrete buildings all around an open yard. I knew that one of those buildings had the gas chamber in it, or the room where they drained the air away and the dogs suffocated to death.

But at least the yard was open, and that's where the dogs were, behind this thick meshed fence. "There he is!" I shouted even before I got out of the car.

That Sam. There he was, only minutes away from extinction, just lying off in one corner, away from the other dogs, having himself a snooze. "Sam!" I called. "Sam!" He heard me and came padding over, with his tail plopping side to side, moderately glad to see me, I guess, because he was grinning. "Thank goodness we're in time!" He knew I wouldn't let him down.

"Woof," said Sam, in that special husky woof that he woofs only to me.

I was just about to ask Dooley to magic a hole in the fence, so Sam could get out, when a man appeared from one of the buildings in the back. I have never liked the idea of dogcatchers in general, but this was the first one I'd ever met—and he was *really* bad news! As big as Frankenstein's monster, and you could tell from that gleam in his eye that he really enjoyed his work.

"Whaddaya want here?" he barked at us. Except dogs sometimes sound nice when they bark. Men don't. "Get away from that fence! You're makin' the animals nervous."

"I want my dog," I said. "This is him. This is Sam."

"Got a license? Got a permit?"

"Sam *has* a license—"

"Got *authorization*? I picked this animal up this mornin'—with specific instructions. Now get outta here!" He dragged Sam off to a bunch of dogs that were cowering against one wall. They must have been the condemned group for that day.

Behind me Dooley softly asked, "Master, shall I make that man vanish?—and I mean *vanish*! Not like Maurice."

"No, no. It's not his fault he's a creep," I said. "At least, don't evaporate him yet." The man had gone into the building. "Gee, I don't know what to do. Even if you get Sam out, I can't bring him home again."

"Well, master," said Dooley, " 'tis my opinion that we should do *something*. I fear that the creep has evil designs on Sam." His forehead puckered up a minute. And then, just as if it weren't a revolutionary solution, he came up with the answer. "Would Aunt Lucy object to Sam if he were not a dog?"

I didn't get him at first. "What else *could* he be?"

"Oh—an insect, a fish—a man."

"Could you make him a *man*—?"

"With a flicker of these fingertips."

"But Dooley—" talk about having your mind blown— "a *man*!"

"I know, little master. But in the sight of these eyes—which are immortal—the difference between an ant and a man is less than human pride might wish."

A man! . . . "Would it hurt?" I asked.

"There *is* pain in being human, but the transformation would cause him none."

"He might not like me any more—"

"I think he will love you, master—though men are less faithful than dogs."

"But how long would he stay a man?"

"As long as my spell held him." Just like that! So matter-of-factly. "Lo, master, the creep comes again."

The dogcatcher had come out of that building and was heading for a dismal little blockhouse off in one corner of the yard. The condemned group knew what was coming, too. They were barking hysterically and running around in circles, in fear.

"Do it, Dooley!" I said. The man's back was turned as he unlocked the door. "Oh, do it—please!"

The Genie lifted his right hand, and from the depths of his chest, he sort of sang, "Oh, simple, soulless beast named Sam—I call thee to the dubious estate—*of man!*"

7

Sam

"Put clothes on him!" I was so shocked I didn't even have time to be amazed.

Because there he was. Naked as a jaybird! Standing amid all those barking dogs, with a look on his face as if he had just dropped down from another planet. Which I suppose, in a way, he had. And it's lucky we live in a time of hair, because he was the whiskeriest man I ever saw.

Dooley made another pass with his right hand, and just-like-that Sam had shoes, brown slacks, a white shirt, and a mottled brown sport jacket on. I haven't described Sam the dog to you in detail, but he was mostly patchy brown and white, and Sam the man really did rather look like him. Of course you'd have to have known them both to see the resemblance.

The dogs were barking even louder now, because they, too, were shocked at what had happened to Sam, and the dogcatcher turned around from unlocking the gas chamber. "Hey!" he shouted. "Who are you?"

Sam yelped a little in his old voice and then got out the words, "I—I'm—I'm a *man*?"

"And whaddaya think you're doin' in here?"

Sam looked at me with this bug-eyed, pleading expression. "Help him, Dooley," I whispered.

The Genie pointed his forefinger at Sam's throat. And automatically out came Sam's voice: "I'm an inspector from the Society for the Prevention of Cruelty to Animals."

"Yeah?—well, we got inspected last month. An' we're clean," said the creep. "Now get outta here! You're makin' the animals nervous."

"I would have been pretty nervous myself," said Sam furiously. "If you know you've got only two minutes to—"

"Get *outta* here!" The guy took Sam by the elbow and

pushed him toward a gate in the fence, which he unbolted from inside. "An' *stay* out!"

And there we were—face to face . . .

"Sam—?" I still didn't really believe.

"Timmy—?" Neither did he.

Then all at once we did! And we were laughing, and Sam lifted me up and swung me back and forth. That was something I'd often done to Sam, when I got big enough to lift him, but this was the first time he'd done it to me and it was a funny experience.

He was still pretty doggy. A lot of his laughter sounded like barking. "Dooley," I said, when Sam put me down, "you've got to fix that voice."

Dooley touched his longest finger to Sam's throat and said, "You canine voice—now hark! Use human accents. And don't bark!" Sam cleared his throat, and after that his voice was better.

"Is everything else okay, Sam?" I asked.

He stretched out a leg. "It feels sort of strange to stand on only two feet. The balance—"

"I know. It takes little kids a long time. Dooley, do you think you could—"

"Legs," said Dooley, "straighten up! And carry Sam with pride. Forget the quadruped inside." I guess that's what you would call instant evolution.

But I was still jittery, staying there by the dog pound. "Come on." I tugged Sam's sleeve. "Let's go."

Sam held back, looking into the yard. "I'm kind of sorry for all those guys. I mean—dogs." His own face looked pretty hangdog and sad. "I got to know a couple of them."

All I had to do was glance at Dooley. It didn't even need a spoken spell. The bolt slid back, and the gate swung open, as nice as pie.

A little terrier saw the escape route first. He couldn't believe his eyes and just gawked a minute. Then he shouted something in dog talk, and in one second there was the wildest, noisiest, furriest stream pouring through that gate that you could ever hope to see.

"Hey wait!" the dogcatcher shouted. "Stop!"

Nobody did, of course. I never found out what happened to all those dogs pouring up and down Houston Street, but I hope they made their way to safety.

In the car—we were all in the front seat, I never did like the idea of a chauffeur plunked up there all by himself—my nose began to twitch. "Gee, Sam, I didn't keep you very clean. You smell half like Aunt Lucy's perfume and half like a dirty kennel. I suppose that's the dog pound."

"Oh, now, Tim," said Sam, "you're not going to give me another bath, are you? We had one just yesterday."

"Why, Sam—" I was rather disappointed—"I thought

you enjoyed them." That was the first time I learned there was more to Sam than Sam.

"Well, I don't," he said. "I put up with them only because I knew you liked them so much."

"But it's different for men." I thought I could coax him into it. "And I'd like a bath, too. Wouldn't you, Dooley?"

"Yes, master!" said Dooley enthusiastically. "I used to visit the Wizard's Chamber of Steaming Delights frequently."

"I think a local Turkish bath will do enough for now," I said.

We found one in midtown and went in. That was really a happy two hours! I'd never been to a steam bath before, with all the white tiles shining. At first I didn't like the steam room—and neither did Sam—but Dooley enjoyed it so much, slapping himself around and dashing from a hot shower into a freezing cold one, that Sam and I caught the fun of it, too.

"How do you like it, Sam?" I asked.

"It's great!" Of course he knew better by now, but he threw back his head and barked for the heck of it.

That brought the bath attendant in. "You got a dog in here?" he asked suspiciously.

"No, sir!" said Sam, very earnest now. "There's nobody here but us humans."

That set the three of us off on a binge of laughing.

They had a swimming pool, too. To begin with, Sam could only do the dog paddle, but in half an hour Dooley and I had him managing the Australian crawl.

Then came cleanup time. Dooley got a razor and scissors from the attendant and gave Sam a shave and a haircut. He still looked pretty scraggly. I asked Dooley why he just didn't do it all by magic, and he said there was no point in doing by magic what you could do by hand. Which makes sense. The only magic he did right then was to snap his fingers and find in one hand a little vial— "containing a very sweet scent," he said, "distilled from the Wizard's spice garden," which he proceeded to slap all over Sam's face. Among other things, Dooley proved to be an excellent barber.

I got to comb Sam's hair. I always liked to brush him— when he was a dog, I mean—and he must have known, because he bent over obediently, and we tried the part on both sides. We all preferred the left. "There!" I said. "Now I call that a handsome man." And he was, too. He still had something of a stomach, but not too much, in my opinion. "It's time to go home."

Sam whimpered dismally.

"Sam, stop that!" I said. "Dooley fixed your voice."

"I know," he groaned, man-style now, "but I'm scared."

"The whole point of making you a man was so I could

still own you. That is—keep you." I felt queasy about owning Sam the man. "I mean—so we could be together. Isn't that right?"

"Yes, Tim."

"What we'll do is, we'll tell Aunt Lucy that you're an old friend of Lorenzo's. Because that's true enough to say, isn't it?"

"Oh, yes!" said Sam. "Ever since that first day when he found me in the garbage can on Bleecker Street."

"Well, we don't need to tell her *that*! There's no point in being too honest. We'll say that Dooley and I just ran into you while we were driving around this morning."

"Do you think she'll like me, Timmy?" Sam was worried. "You know—as a man?"

"I don't know, Sam," I said. "But I hope you make a better impression than you did as a dog."

During the drive back to Sutton Place we all were quiet. The Cadillac was full of Sam's anxiety.

And in the elevator, I remembered something else. "Sam, you have to have a last name. What one do you want?"

He thought a moment—desperately, you could see by his face. Then he said, "Oh—Bassinger, I guess."

That struck me as funny—and also pretty original. "Why Bassinger, Sam?"

"You never knew it, Timmy," said Sam, "but my father was a basset hound, and my mother was a springer spaniel."

8

The Fearful Lunch

Aunt Lucy was in the living room. "Oh, Timmy—I've been so worried"—as usual. She was worried last night, she was worried this morning—she did a lot of worrying in those days. "I didn't know where—" Then she saw Sam behind me.

For a minute I thought the impossible: that she recognized him. Her forehead and eyes pinched into a question. But then they smoothed out clear again.

Sam, of course, was just standing there with that basset expression of pure dumb hopeless love.

Things had to be joggled on. I rushed into the silence that was holding us all apart. "Aunt Lucy, this is Mr. Bassinger. He's an old friend of Lorenzo's and mine; we met him this morning driving around, and since he's an old friend of Lorenzo's and mine, I thought I'd—I thought I'd—" About here I ran out of steam.

But Aunt Lucy came to my rescue. "You thought you'd bring him up to say hello." She smiled.

"That's *right*!" I said.

"I'm so glad you did. How do you do, Mr. Bassinger?" She held out her hand.

I breathed an inward sigh of relief that I'd taught Sam how to shake hands. But he did it like a dog. Just held his hand out limply and waited for Aunt Lucy to take it, shake it, and then let it go again. It's funny how something like a limp handshake can be so appealing in a dog, but kind of icky in a man.

"Well—" Aunt Lucy began to jitter, because Sam still hadn't said a word—"I *am* glad to meet a friend of Timmy's."

I was beginning to fear for his voice myself, when he managed to get out, "I'm pleased to meet you, Miss Farr. Again."

"Oh? Have we met before?" said Aunt Lucy.

"I told him all about you, Aunt Lucy." I realized right then that I was going to have to pay careful attention to everything and do a lot of tidying up.

"Mr. Bassinger—" Aunt Lucy's voice went into its social register—"I have an idea. It's past time for lunch—I was waiting for Timmy—do say that you'll stay and have luncheon with us."

"Luncheon?" Sam looked at me with terrorized eyes. You'd have thought she'd said rabies shots. "At the *table*—?"

Fortunately she misunderstood. "Perhaps you're one of those very courageous people who don't eat lunch—" For those whole great weeks we were saved very often by somebody's ignorance.

"Usually I have just one meal a day," said Sam. "And two biscuits when I wake up."

"Won't you make an exception this noon?" said Aunt Lucy, flirting with his appetite. "We're having lamb chops—"

"Lamb chops—" I could see Sam's mouth begin to water.

"Oh, good! You do like them."

"I like the bones—"

I gave a warning cough to Sam. The first of many warning coughs. By the end of that lunch, Aunt Lucy was sure I had a cold, and I *had* made my throat sore.

"I'll ask Rose to set another place." Aunt Lucy went into the kitchen.

"Timmy," Sam yowled, "take me back to the dog pound!"

"Now, Sam—" I wanted to pet his head. But apart from being caught by Aunt Lucy, I guessed all those doggy things were now out.

"I can't make it, Tim! I can't!"

"Yes you can, Sam. Just keep watching me."

"I'm a dog—"

"No you're *not*! You're a man. You've got to put all that behind you, Sam. When you're in doubt—look at me. And I'll—I'll—" As a matter of fact, I didn't know *what* I'd do, but I had to put up a good front, for Sam—"I'll give you little lessons in elemental humanity."

Sam threw back his head, about to howl, but Aunt Lucy came in and he managed to stifle it.

"We'll only be a few minutes more. Won't you sit down, Mr. Bassinger?"

Now Aunt Lucy took over. That's one thing about living in Sutton Place: you learn how to make an awful lot of idiotic but very useful small talk. And Aunt Lucy really did her duty that day. She could see that Sam was very nervous—as well he might be: except for the car this was the first time he'd ever sat up in a chair—and to set him at ease she let go a Mississippi of chatter. About the plays she liked. And the operas. And all the committees she was on. And me—what *fun* having me living there! It was all dull stuff, but she did it for Sam, just out of politeness. That was the first time I realized how important boring conversation can be. People's lives just slide along on it.

Sam *was* edgy! Just as if he had fleas. (I think we got rid of the last of them in the Turkish bath.) At one point he began to scratch his ear. Of course he couldn't use his leg, the way a dog would use his right hind leg, but the same quick jerky motions were there. I gave another warning cough. But I'm not going to put down all my coughs, it would sound too much like tuberculosis.

Rose came in and announced, "Lunch, Miss Lucy." She had a way of not sounding like a servant—only someone who had an announcement to make . . .

And the fearful luncheon began . . .

When poor Sam saw the fork, the knife, and the spoons, you'd have thought they were going to be used to carve him up, instead of the lamb chops. In very slow motion I opened my napkin and spread it in my lap. Sam did the same. I had hopes for his table manners, because he was usually a very neat dog. Although his tail was clumsy sometimes, he never slobbered around his bowl or left a mess. So little by little, secretively, and with many a glance in my direction, Sam learned how to use the utensils. Fork like this—knife like this—carve *slowly*!—et cetera . . .

Rose served us the courses, one by one—tomato juice first—and behind the swinging door to the kitchen I could see Dooley spying. He had his widest smile on, because he knew the crazy truth of everything that was happening.

Meanwhile, Aunt Lucy was pouring out her torrent of necessary nonsense. When I wasn't concentrating on Sam, I was thanking her silently.

Dessert arrived—almost a disaster! Because you know how much dogs like ice cream. Sam's face lit up, and I thought he was going to lean right over and lap. But I managed, accidentally, to bang my spoon on my water glass, and he smartened up and used his spoon.

We moved into the living room. That's a custom they have up in Sutton Place: you take your coffee somewhere else. It's a nice custom, too, because it's fun to change places for the last part of a meal.

I was feeling very self-satisfied. Here was my dog—I mean, my ex-dog—sipping demitasse in the company of my aunt, and I thought to myself, This can't have happened to *too* many other kids.

Then Rose came in with the bad news. "Miss Lucy, Mr. Watkins is here."

"Oh, lovely! I wasn't expecting him yet. He can join us for coffee."

Sam bristled.

It's different when a man bristles. His hair doesn't stand up quite so high, but it stands up high enough to make somebody worry.

"Henry," said Aunt Lucy in that phony high but workable tone she'd been using through lunch, "this is **Mr.**

Bassinger. A friend of Lorenzo's. And of Timmy, too!"
She glittered at me, to prove her point.

" 'Ullo," said Sam, in a bassety voice. He gave Mr.
Watkins a limp handshake. I hated that. Because I knew
Sam was really a strong dog. Or man. Or whatever he was.
At that stage I wasn't really sure.

Aunt Lucy began churning out more chatter, but Mr.
Watkins wouldn't go along with fluff. I could see that he
instinctively didn't like Sam, just as much as Sam resented
him. It was chemical, that's all. He kept digging in.

Like—"What's your field, Bassinger?"

"Well, I—I— " Sam looked to me for help. But I didn't
have any.

"Between jobs, eh?" Mr. Watkins lit a cigarette. He did it
as if he'd scored a point. "Kind of late to change horses,
isn't it?"

"Am I going to change horses?" Sam panicked at me. I
shut my eyes and shook my head a little, to reassure him: no.

"The recession, I meant," said Mr. Watkins. "And a
man your age, to be changing careers. What line of work
have you been in?"

"Just—mostly—" Sam gave another quick scratch at his
ear, but then remembered and held his hand in his lap
—"prowling around, I guess."

"Prowling?" Old Watkins wouldn't let that go by.

"I mean—inspecting is more what I do."

"Inspecting *what*?"

"Oh—trees—fireplugs—"

"I see. A city job," sneered Mr. Watkins cattily.

That's it! I didn't realize it till now, but Mr. Watkins was a cat person.

Don't misunderstand: I've met some very nice cat people. Mrs. Libovski, who owned the clock shop next to Madame Sosostris's on Bleecker Street, was definitely a cat woman. I don't just mean she owned cats—she did, three Siamese —I mean, if she'd been an animal, she would have been a cat. I think inside of everybody, along with the humanity, there exists a possible animal. I don't mean like the dog in Sam—a transformation like that must take place only once in a very blue moon. I mean, more like what that person might have been. For instance Aunt Lucy: there's a little nervous squirrel sitting up on its hind legs inside of her. And Dooley—he'd have been, perhaps not a bull or a bear, but something big and dark and powerful. Rose has a panther inside her, but a quiet one, with its tail switched around its legs—only don't make her mad.

And if ever there was a man with a cat—a *catty* cat, not like one of Mrs. Libovski's—inside of him it was Henry Watkins.

I can see now that that explained Sam's reaction. His lips began to curl, and I heard a growl coming up from his chest.

Mr. Watkins didn't help things, either, by asking Aunt

Lucy, right over my head, "How did the chappy take his
—canine separation this morning?" As if any kid doesn't
know what "canine" means.

The squirrel in Aunt Lucy twitched nervously at me.
"Uh—we haven't discussed it, Henry."

"What canine separation?" snarled Sam.

"Tim had this dog—a pretty ragged character—that
didn't fit in. I'm proud of the way you're accepting this,
Tim—"

He didn't have time to finish his purring compliment,
because Sam barked, "Yes, and *you're* the one who called
the dogcatcher—!"

"How did *you* know that?"

"A *guess!*" Sam's teeth were all out now.

We were right on the edge of a downright cat-and-dog
fight.

"Mr. Bassinger—" I stood up—"would you like to see
my room? I have some things of Lorenzo's there."

Sam got his dog under control and muttered, "Yes, I
would. Very much."

It turned out that Aunt Lucy and Mr. Watkins were
going off to a meeting of the Committee for the Preserva-
tion of the Upper East Side. But before they left, Aunt
Lucy made a point of shaking hands with Sam again and
said, "It's been such fun to have you to lunch. Will you
come another time?"

"I'd like to, Miss Farr," Sam mumbled.

" 'Miss Farr' is so formal. My first name's Lucy—" Sam didn't say anything. "And yours is—?"

Sam looked, hangdog, at his feet and said, "Sam."

"Sam—" Aunt Lucy flicked her eyes at me. And then giggled. "Well, *that's* a coincidence!"

Again I wondered, like in Mr. Dickinson's office, if all coincidences, if you got to know the whole truth about them, are just as complicated and planned as this one was.

In my bedroom I tried to cool Sam down. He still was fuming and woofing indignantly. "He *did* call the dog-catcher, Timmy. He was here at the crack of dawn." I wanted to hold him in my lap—but no way.

Dooley came in, with a pumpkin grin. "How fares our former quadruped, master?"

"Pretty primitive, Dooley," I said. "As if you didn't know! Eavesdropping in the hall like that. Does Rose suspect anything?"

"She suspects something, master. But she knows not what she suspects. Her only comment, whispered to me in the kitchen after Sam had sniffed at the salad, was, 'There's something funny about that man.' "

"She doesn't know the half of it," I said.

"Ah, Sam—do the nets of human nature ensnare thee?"

"I'll say," said Sam dejectedly.

Dooley put his arm around Sam's shoulder and squeezed: a man-to-man gesture. Pretty strange when you think that one was a genie, just let out of a rug, and the other, two hours ago, was a dog.

"I don't have a job—" Sam looked down sadly at the foot of my bed. "I can't sleep in my box any more—"

"Fear not, Sam. For I can provide any lodging you wish."

"And as far as work goes, Sam," I said, "isn't there something you'd like to do?"

"No! I was happy the way I was. Scrounging is fun. Timmy—" he looked at me with a pleading hopelessness —"maybe I better go back to—"

"No!" It was my turn to put my foot down. "You *have* to give it a try, Sam—you have to! Just think."

"Think," grumped Sam, disgusted.

" 'Tis the task of man, Sam," said Dooley philosophically.

Sam shook his head. "When I woke up this morning, the biggest problem I had was to choose between Alpo and Chuck Wagon."

But then he did try to think. Dooley and I helped him silently.

And something worked. Because Sam broke out in a big laugh and said, "Hey!—*there is* something that I ought to be good at!"

9

Sam's Pet Shop

That's what the sign over the door said—in big beautiful letters that Dooley invented.

It was on Second Avenue, and Sam and Dooley had their apartments—floor-throughs—on the second and third floor above. On the top floor lived Mr. Cantarell. He was one of those Collier-brother-type recluses who don't go out for anything except to get food. And right in the middle of the biggest, busiest city in the world! I met him

in the hall once and I liked him, but he doesn't have anything to do with anything—so there he still lives.

When I learned, the day after the nervous lunch, that
Sam had his pet shop and that Dooley and he had acquired
pads, coincidentally, in the very same building on Second
Avenue, I began to worry about evaporated former
tenants. But Dooley swore to me that he hadn't done anything to anyone. It was kind of a rickety building, down
in the twenties, and all vacant, except for Mr. Cantarell.
They kept him on, at his same cheap rent, for charity, and
because he liked animals.

The way they got it was, Dooley made money. And I
mean he really made money! About twenty-five thousand
dollars in one afternoon. (That's another thing: if anybody should find some fake money around, hold on to it.
It may be Dooley's, and it'll probably be very precious
someday. There can't be too much counterfeit in circula-
tion that a genie himself created.)

But after the money they did it all themselves. That
same business about not wasting magic on what you can do
by hand. Once the building was bought, and the mortgage
arranged—with some doctored credentials for Sam—they
tore through the place like two hurricanes: painting, scrub-
bing, renovating. Every old building should be so lucky
as to have two guys like Dooley and Sam in it. They even
bought ladders and painted the outside, too. And the

plumbing—all new pipes—everything . . . Believe me, it's lucky that all of that work was really *work*! It lasted beyond the spell.

In two weeks Sam's Pet Shop was ready. And the best time in my life began . . . We started to get the animals.

We decided right off that we wouldn't specialize in just one type. We'd have dogs and cats and fishes and birds and monkeys—and every kind of animal that could possibly find a home in New York. And at that very first conference we also resolved that we'd have special kennels and pens for mongrels and other mixed-together things that the other pet shops might consider just throwaways . . . After all, Sam was no pureblood himself.

I wish it had taken months and months—the fun we had! We began in other pet shops, picking out the animals we liked. Sam would say something like, "I think I could be a friend to that cat."

Or Dooley would say, "A most appealing guppy, master."

Of course I agreed to everything.

But then, after we got the rare guys like the kinkajou and the one we called William Rhesus, we found that on the streets, despite the dogcatchers, cat catchers, and catchers of everything else, there are lots of animals walking around. Sam had the idea of going back to the Houston Street dog pound, to see if we could salvage any of his former friends. We picked up a couple of dogs down there, but I'm not sure whether they were part of Sam's lot.

I found a stray kitten, and, to my surprise, I liked it very much—which shows it only takes a little exposure.

Then, alas, in only a week the shop was all stocked. Except for Felix.

And Felix I've got to tell you about. He was our parakeet.

Dooley came marching in one afternoon, with an especially gleeful grin, and perched on the shoulder of his green chauffeur's uniform was this little green parakeet. "A new addition, gentlemen," said Dooley, with his grin in his voice, too. "I believe we shall call him Felix."

Now "cute" is a word I really hate, but this just had to be the cutest little bird in the world. But with a *wicked* sense of humor! Felix took one look at Sam, and the feathers on the back of his neck stood up; he leaned forward warily and squawked, "You *can* teach an old dog new tricks."

That was the beginning of it. Felix ribbed Sam about his—his past, shall we say—all summer long. I'm sure Dooley taught him what to say; some of it was only repetition. But he also kept coming up with things that could only have been implanted by magic. Dooley never would admit it, though. Whenever Felix came out with one of his cracks, Dooley would only raise his eyebrows and say something like, "By the Wizard's beard!—what a perceptive bird."

For instance, there was the first time Sam got up the courage to ask Aunt Lucy to come around and see his pet shop. Aunt Lucy was doing all the right things—she was "ooing" and "ahing" and stroking the kittens and making a fuss about the puppies—and Sam was just lapping it up, when all of a sudden Felix burst out singing, "You ain't nothin' but a hound dog!"

Now how could a parakeet have learned a very old song like that unless a genie had taught it to him?

Then there was the incident of the lady who couldn't decide which dog biscuits to buy. (I forgot to tell you— we sold food for animals, too.) And Sam forgot himself, as he sometimes did, and said, "Personally, I prefer this brand. It tastes much bet—" He remembered then and blushed.

But Felix wouldn't let him get away with it. Up on his perch he shrieked indignantly, "Why, Sam!—you old dog, you! *Aw haw!*"

I had to go into the bathroom in back and laugh myself out. The lady was gone when I got back—thinking Lord knows what!—but Sam was still furious and bawling Felix out. Felix didn't care a darn. He just made his feathers stand up and squawked in that parroty voice of his, "*Aw haw!* His bark is worse than his bite."

Felix and I established a very good relationship. Of course it wasn't as good as Sam's relationship to all the other animals—because that was something absolutely wonderful. Whenever a puppy had a stomachache or a kitten was teething, Sam knew it instinctively. That, I suppose, was to be expected. But he even related to the fish! And when it came time for shots for someone, Sam would give an injection and not cause a whimper. The little guys were scared of the needle, and Sam remembered how it was . . . Apart from the fun we had in those days, I remember the most beautiful thing of all was the way Sam loved and tended his animals.

But Felix and I had a great friendship, too. I think we were about as tight together as a bird and a boy can get. At first Sam was sort of growly and jealous when Felix and I would fool around. But then he adjusted to it all right. He knew that even as a man he still came first with me.

After days and days of cajoling and coaxing, I got Felix so trusting that he'd sit on my shoulder. Dooley was the only other one that he'd do that for. And Dooley wasn't around all that much after he, Sam, and I had gotten the pet shop in working order. I thought it was just that Aunt Lucy was wasting his time by having him drive her around. He *was* her chauffeur, after all. Though I don't think she really wanted a chauffeur—it was one of those habits left over from Grampa Lorenzo. But there was a lot more to it than Dooley and the Cadillac (which he *had* learned to drive by now), as I found out shortly, to my sorrow.

In the meantime, Felix trusted me enough to sit on my shoulder. And Sam refused to sell him. One day a man came in the shop, when Felix happened to be singing opera, and offered a very extravagant price for him. Sam took one look at my face and said politely, "I'm sorry, that bird is not for sale."

I thought it was very sweet of him, but Felix, with his sense of humor, had to scream out, "A man's best friend is—!"

"Shut up, you green fiend," muttered Sam.

We unloaded a couple of middle-aged canaries on that customer. (They *were* very melodious.) The man that sold them to us said they'd always been together, so we wouldn't separate them.

With Felix the best day came when I went out to the delicatessen to buy some roast-beef sandwiches for Sam and me. (By now you can see that I was spending all day, every day, in the shop.) Felix was sitting on my shoulder, clucking and muttering in parakeet talk, and not even planning what I was doing, I risked it: I walked out the door with him still sitting next to my ear.

He didn't budge. He was good as gold. The fun of it was to walk down Second Avenue, with this dapper green parakeet perched up there, and pretend there was nothing unusual. I kept a dopey normal face and made believe nothing was happening. But the stares, and the grins, and the laughs we got!

In the delicatessen, before I could even say a word, Felix spouted out, "Two roast-beef sandwiches. One on rye with lettuce and mayo."

That was what Sam had said. (I hadn't decided, when we'd left the shop.) Another thing about that parakeet: his memory was phenomenal.

It was kind of a turning point between Felix and me, that walk in the street to get those sandwiches. On the way back, for no reason at all, he moved over close to my ear and whispered—if a parakeet can whisper—"Hello there! Hello there, Tim."

It's really amazing—how animals know what you want to hear. Or feel. When Sam was a dog, when I was down, he'd know it right away and come and put his head in my lap. And Felix knew, on that walk back to the shop, with all the people gawking at us, that I wanted him to talk to me personally.

I began to take him back to the apartment in Sutton Place with me. Aunt Lucy was pretty jittery the first time I walked in with Felix on my shoulder, but she still was feeling guilt-ridden about Sam—not that she'd admit it, of course—so she jittered herself into accepting my new pet. I bought a perch and spread newspapers under it, and Felix just eased himself into the family.

I needed his company, too. You've only heard the good times of the opening-pet-shop weeks, but there were some bad things happening in the background, too, which I tried, unsuccessfully, to ignore.

The worst was my testing. Aunt Lucy and Mr. Watkins couldn't decide which grade I belonged in, and I wasn't about to help them make up their minds. So I got tested . . . Did I ever get tested! For one whole morning I answered questions—written, which I didn't mind, and oral—to this guy who I think was a psychiatrist. To me he looked like a dogcatcher for people.

It turned out that I did *extremely* well in reading and pretty well in math, but I flunked social studies. The psychiatrist decided that I didn't relate to "my peer group" at all—that means kids my own age—and it's completely untrue. (The only reason that Jimmy Libovski and Irving Siesel don't come into what happened is that they had no part in it.) The shrink recommended a dose of summer camp . . . This was still only July, and I had all of August to learn how to relate.

Aunt Lucy was only too glad to hear her worst suspicions confirmed. Ever since I'd been living with her, she'd been beefing—no, fidgeting—about my not having any

friends my own age. Well, it's true. Since I'd moved up to
Sutton Place, my friends were a very good singer who was
earning money as a cook, a genie disguised as a chauffeur,
a medium in Greenwich Village, a man who used to be
my dog, and a parakeet with a sharp sense of humor . . .
In my opinion, these were friends enough.

The worst was the testing, but more subtle and more
dangerous were those duets.

They began one sweltering day—this must have been
about three weeks ago—when Dooley came back from
having deposited Aunt Lucy at some very important civic
gathering. He was sweating like a horse, and despite all the
air conditioning, which there's plenty of in our apartment,
Rose suggested that he take a shower.

"A most comfortable idea," said Dooley, and he did a
little bow . . . He was always doing things, like bowing,
or calling her "Rose of the petal lips," that turned her on,
although she didn't know what to make of them.

So off Dooley went to Rose's bathroom. But he didn't
take a shower—he took a bath. You know what a bathtub
does for a voice: if you sound good in the living room,
you'll sound like the Met in the tub. And if that happens
to a *man*, you can just imagine what happens to a genie's
voice.

He was singing a song that I think was in Arabic. As
soon as Rose and I, who were just about to have lunch,

heard the sounds that were coming from that throat, we put down our sandwiches quietly, not wanting to chew, and just blinked at each other. He definitely was a baritone, but he had a tenor's top and the luscious low notes of a bass . . . Music is one of the very few ways that magic gets into humanity. When you hear a great voice, you almost want to stop breathing, to listen.

He came back in a few minutes, looking refreshed but as if nothing at all had happened. Rose was gawking up at him, and she said, "Man, have *you* got a voice! Where did you learn to sing like that?"

Dooley looked surprised. Sometimes he didn't know where his gifts really were. "But, Mistress Rose, all things beneath the sun love to sing."

"Well, all things beneath the sun don't sing like *that*! You know any spirituals?"

"Spirituals?"

"Sure. They always want us to sing spirituals—until we can prove that we really know how to sing."

"Then sing me a spiritual," said Dooley, with his voice inviting, and ingratiating, and sly.

Rose launched into "Deep River"—"Deep river, my soul lies over Jordan"—et cetera. It's my favorite. I'd heard her practicing it for weeks, but she knew that she was in front of a master now, and she sang it especially well.

But Dooley had to do some teasing. "Oh, Mistress Rose,"

he scoffed, "that river—the Jordan—'tis not so deep. I've swum in it—"

Rose exploded. "I don't care if you've *swum* in it. Can you *sing* it?—that's all."

He'd only heard it that once, but Dooley straight off sang a rendition of "Deep River" the like of which couldn't have been heard in many kitchens in Sutton Place before.

"Man—!" Rose was absolutely goggle-eyed by now. "You're wasting your time in that chauffeur's uniform! I'm taking you straight to my teacher—"

Which she did . . . And that was the beginning of Dooley's singing lessons . . . Also those ducts. Rose's vocalizing had a baritone accompaniment to it now.

I was so happy during all of those weeks I forgot to think. If I'd put everything together—especially what Dooley said the first night that I conjured him—I could have expected the coming catastrophe. But no. There I was, drifting along in bliss in Sam's pet shop, having a ball every day, and totally unaware of how thin the ice of magic is. Especially when it comes up against something as strong as the longings of human nature.

It began to happen, the disaster did, one Friday afternoon. Sam was dithering around, the way he always dithered when Aunt Lucy was coming to visit—which she did more and more often these days.

Felix wasn't helping much. Whenever Sam would nervously ask me if I thought the puppies' cages were clean enough, Felix would laugh—"Aw haw!"—and rasp out something like, "There's a dog in this manger."

"Felix, if you don't shut up—!"

"Now, now, Sam." I tried to soothe his hackles down. I felt them there, underneath his collar, even though they weren't as obvious as when he was a dog. "You just keep on cleaning—I'll take care of Felix."

"You better!" Sam growled. "Because I'm gonna bust him one—"

"Distemper! That's what it is!" shrieked Felix. "Get the vet," he ordered gloomily. "It may be contagious."

I got him, finally, to shut his beak by giving him a cracker. Although he never would stoop to that dopey pollywannacracker routine.

Aunt Lucy arrived—looking a lot more spiffy than she needed to, just visiting a friend in his pet shop.

"Hi, Lucy!" Sam grinned sheepishly.

"Hi, Sam." Aunt Lucy grinned right back. And the squirrel in her giggled.

"I've got the carrots all ready—"

"Fun! Let's start."

It seems that Aunt Lucy had developed a passion for the rabbits. She just *loved* to come over every afternoon and give them their supper. Believe me, rabbits are not bright animals. They're lovable, but unobservant, and they

don't know the difference between a Bergdorf Goodman
suit and a pair of overalls.

While Aunt Lucy was squealing her joy at "how the
bunnies love to nibble," and Sam was standing there, passing her carrots obediently, Felix and I went over to visit
with William Rhesus. At that point the company of a
monkey felt very refreshing. We talked to him for a
while, and I think he understood. But you never can tell
with monkeys. They're tricky, being almost up to man.

Then we drifted over to the puppy cage, which is where
we usually end up. It's my favorite place in the shop.
Everybody recognized me, jumped up on their hind legs,
forepaws on the screen, and started barking. I love that
shrill little pitiful bark that puppies have.

Sam came over with Lucy and said to the puppies, "Now
settle down, men—settle down."

"I wasn't doing anything to upset them, Sam," I said.

"I know, Tim. Those are just love barks. But they get
too excited."

"You ought to know!" Felix muttered under his breath.

"A parakeet can be fricasseed, too!" growled Sam,
under his.

Aunt Lucy cooed at the puppies awhile. Then her face
got this curious rueful expression. "Why look, Timmy,"
she said. "That brown and white one—over in the corner—
he looks just like—"

It was true. And Aunt Lucy had noticed it even before

I had. In the new batch there was one little mongrel guy who had exactly Sam's coloring. I think there was basset in him somewhere, too. He looked so forlorn and intimidated, meeting all those new strange people and dogs— this was his very first day, after all—that I had to reach in and pick him up. Sam looked at the puppy sympathetically and then took him in his own arms.

"Who does he look like, Lucy?" said Sam in a very quiet voice.

She hesitated, glanced fidgetily at me—we hadn't talked about it in the open yet, since that first day of Sam's being a man—and said, "Tim had this dog who couldn't adapt to life with us in Sutton Place—and Timmy bravely gave him up. You *have* been good about that, too, dear!" She gave my hand a squeeze—which *felt* like a squeeze this time.

"Um—well—Aunt Lucy," I hemmed and didn't know what to say. So I hawed, "It hasn't been too hard."

"*You've* been a help there, Sam," said Aunt Lucy. "You've been such a friend to my nephew."

"A man's best friend—" began Felix ominously.

"Quiet!" I commanded him. He'll obey me, although he won't Sam.

"You didn't like him at all?" Sam asked sadly, in a voice unlike his usual happy-go-lucky human woofing, which bore a resemblance to his dog voice.

"You know," Aunt Lucy admitted, after a minute, "I

really did. I'd grown quite fond of Sam. He was terribly
clumsy, though—"

Right here—and wouldn't you know he'd do it?—Sam
leaned against the puppies' cage and knocked it over.
Nobody was hurt, but all of them scattered like furry
drops of rain around the shop.

When we'd rounded them up, Aunt Lucy continued,
enjoying her nostalgia now that there was no work involved: "Yes, I *had* grown fond of Sam. He'd stare at me
with such *feeling* in that woebegone face—!"

Sam stared at the floor, to hide his woebegone. "He must
have liked you an awful lot."

Then it happened.

I could see Sam was losing control—and did my nerves
ever tighten me up!—but I was expecting, if anything, that
he'd lick her hand or lift his paws—I mean, his hands—to
her shoulders and start to bark rhapsodically. But it was
worse than either one.

He howled.

I think he meant to say something fairly icky, but instead of words, this pitiful canine howl came out. A man's
voice is one of his very most human characteristics, and
when Sam started to relapse, his voice went first. He stared
at me, terrified. Aunt Lucy couldn't believe her ears and
looked down in the puppy cage, thinking the sound must
have come from there.

Sam cleared his throat and tried to say something. But

now he only halfheartedly woofed. His eyes got big as they pleaded with me—to make it stop, or at least explain what was happening. And Aunt Lucy knew by this time that Sam was making those noises. But naturally—and thank God!—not knowing the truth, she expected some rational explanation.

I came up with the only one I could find. And pretty idiotic, too. I said, "Sam, some of that puppy's fur must have gotten into your throat." He was still holding his duplicate. "You're coughing badly. Better put him down. And *try not to speak for a while!*"

Sam's eyes understood, and he put the puppy back into the cage, tapping his throat all the while and smiling at Aunt Lucy, as if it were all very natural . . . Natural!

"We'd better be getting back, Aunt Lucy," I said unhurriedly.

"Well, but if Sam's not well—"

"Oh, it happens all the time when you own a pet shop. Doesn't it, Sam?"

He nodded as cheerfully as he could, over his panic, and motioned us hopefully toward the door.

After a few more Sutton Place pleasantries, I managed to get Aunt Lucy out.

We took a cab back home—where I meant to ask that genie just exactly what was happening!

10

Back to the Occult Sciences

He was in my room, lounging all over my bed. He filled it
to overflowing, too. Since coming to work for Aunt Lucy,
Dooley had gotten into the habit of making my room his
headquarters . . . When he wasn't vocalizing with Rose,
that is.

"What are you looking so dreamy about?" I demanded.

"Nothing, master." He sat up. "Am I looking dreamy?"

"Yes!" I explained what had happened as unexcitedly
as I could.

He stroked his chin and murmured, "Very strange."

"Is that all you can say—'Very strange'? Sam's on the way back to dogville! Now what about that spell of yours?"

"Master," he asked reflectively, "when did all this happen?"

"About fifteen minutes ago." He said nothing. "Dooley—?" His silence began to get worrying. "What were *you* doing fifteen minutes ago?"

"Mistress Rose was teaching me a most lovely French song." He began to sing—as if nothing at all had happened—"*Plaisir d'amour*," "The Pleasure of Love."

It was pretty, too. But I was in no mood for French songs. "Dooley, be *serious*! What's going on?"

"I know not, master. But I suspect." He paced up and down for a minute or two; then said, "Master, where did you find the blessed spell that released me from my exquisite prison?"

"In my father's diary. Why?"

"We must consult his books again."

"But *Sam*—he's—"

"Just one moment, master." He closed his eyes and concentrated, tightening up the spell, I guess. "That ought to hold our furry friend."

"And don't joke! This is critical."

"Pardon, master." He smiled down all over me. "But the whimsicality of mortal life begins to affect me, I fear."

We took Felix with us. Because I needed all the moral support I could get.

In half an hour we were down in the Village. But the CLOSED sign was in the antique-shop window.

"At this hour of the afternoon that can only mean she's holding a séance. Come on around to the back," I said. (There's a rear entrance, too—down an alley and into the kitchen.) We crept in silently. "Oh, Lord—it's the Willy sisters! This'll take all day."

Dooley peeked through the curtains into the séance room. There they sat: Edna and Emma Willy, still trying to get in touch with their sister Nelly, who had died a couple of years before. A very difficult case for Madame Sosostris, because they just wouldn't stop believing in her, and that made her feel guilty whenever she failed—which she did, once a month, when they came around.

"Master," Dooley whispered to me, with mischief in his voice, "shall we make this a truly memorable séance for Madame Sosostris and the Willy sisters?"

"Now look, Dooley, we're not down here to have—"

"Peace, master! It will also save time."

"Well—oh, all right!" I have to admit, despite my fears for Sam, I wasn't averse to a little fun. "Are you going to get the Spirits down?"

Dooley suddenly looked serious. "No, master. The Spirits *do* exist—but I have no traffic whatsoever with them. They come from an altogether different quarter of all the possible universe. Blessed be their rest!" His face got back to its grin again. "Still, I believe that I may enhance the proceedings a little."

I explained the situation to him, while Madame Sosostris went into her spiel—in her most mediumistic voice—"Oh, ye great Spirits who guard the entrance to the Infinite Void, I call on you to reveal yourselves!"

"Now she sets off the Fiendish Laughter," I whispered.

In the spooky light from the Tiffany lamp we could make out Madame Sosostris's right foot, feeling for the Fiendish button . . . when all of a sudden this huge deep laughter burst out all over the séance table! . . . I suppose that it shouldn't have come as a surprise that a genie was also a great ventriloquist, but it did.

Madame Sosostris was pretty rattled. She repeated skeptically, "I—I call on you to reveal yourselves—"

Another booming laugh! . . .

"What?" Emma Willy, who was hard of hearing, cupped her hand to her ear. "What's she saying?"

"She's asking who it is," shouted Edna in awe, as if she'd rather have whispered it.

The biggest, deepest laughter yet!

"It's not Nelly!" Emma shook her head.

"Who—uh—who are you?" asked Madame Sosostris nervously to the empty air.

"I am the Guardian of Blessed Souls!" boomed out Dooley.

"What'd he say?" Emma cupped her ear.

"He says he's the Guardian of Blessed Souls!"

"Oh, well, that's nice." Emma relaxed. "That means she made it at least."

"Doctor—I mean, Guardian—is there—is there anyone there?"

"Now she sets off Lulu," I whispered to Dooley. "It's apparition time."

Before Madame S. had time to touch the Lulu button, Dooley flicked his fingers—and a cloud of white vapor materialized above the séance table.

"Holy smoke!" Madame Sosostris jerked back and almost lost her turban.

"What'd she say?"

"She says it's the holy smoke!"

"That's it! It's ectoplasm!" Madame S. was really out of her tree by now. "I'm havin' a breakthrough!"

"Now take it easy, Dooley," I said. "We don't want her going bananas—"

"Peace, master—and leave this séance to me."

"I call on you, Guardian!" said Madame Sosostris authoritatively—she was into it now—"Is anyone there who wishes to speak to the Willy sisters?"

"Only me." I'd never have believed it, but Dooley was doing falsetto now, and he sounded just like an elderly but likable sister.

"Nelly!" screamed Edna. *"It's Nelly!"*

"That's nice," said Emma. "Tell her hello, and then ask her what in tarnation she did with the keys to the downstairs closet."

Dooley closed his eyes—ransacking the Willy sisters' apartment mentally—then opened them, winked at me, and said, in the same old-lady voice, "They're under the bathroom mat."

"Well, *that's* a silly place to hide anything!" exclaimed Edna. "Did you hear that, sister?"

"No." Emma cupped her ear. When Edna repeated the information, at the top of her lungs, Emma said, "The floors are *your* job, dear. If you cleaned a little more often, we would have found them by now."

"Of all the nerve! *My* job—"

Dooley, in character, chipped right into the argument. "It seems to me that since I've been gone the whole apartment's turned into a mess."

"Nelly Willy," said Edna, "just who do you think you are? Just because you're dead—"

I had to laugh. There they were—bickering together lovingly—just the same as when all three were alive. The two sisters left had only wanted to contact Nelly to have another friendly fight . . . It's true: people never do change.

"Cut it short," I whispered to Dooley. "We've got to get at those books."

He nodded and crooned, "Ooo—I'm fading—ooo—" And the mist above the table began to disappear.

"Nelly?—you leaving?"

"Ooo—yes!" moaned Dooley deliciously. "It's back to the heavenly pastures for me."

"Emma!—say goodbye to Nelly."

" 'Bye, Nelly!"

The mist vanished completely.

"Wasn't it grand to see Nelly again?" Edna dabbed at her eyes with an old silk handkerchief.

"What?" Emma said.

"Oh, forget it. Come on, let's go home. Madame Sosostris, this is by far the best séance we've had."

"Boy, I'll say!" Madame Sosostris was sitting there in a daze.

Edna took out her beat-up antique purse. "The usual fee is two dollars—"

"Forget it. This one's on me."

"That's very kind of you. *Come on, will you?* We'll be back again next month."

Madame Sosostris gazed up where the smoke had been. "I only hope Nelly will, too."

The sisters drifted out through the antique shop, with

many expressions of friendship, and thanks, and elderly affection. Madame Sosostris just kept sitting there, amazed at what she thought she'd done.

I bustled in. "Hi, Madame S.! We came in through the back—"

"Timmy!" We hadn't seen each other since Sam opened his pet shop. "I thought you'd given up on me."

"Oh—Madame Sosostris—" amid magic, pleasure, and everything else, there was also a small place to be ashamed —"you didn't really think that. You know I—"

"Sure, sure, I know." She whacked my shoulder. "You should have been here! I've just had— Who's this?"

"He's Dooley!" I said, with a little too much enthusiasm. "I mean—he's Aunt Lucy's new chauffeur." Even with her, I didn't want to blow his cover. "Dooley—Madame Sosostris."

"Mistress—" He did his little bow.

"Hi, Dooley!" But Madame Sosostris is an American medium. She stuck out her hand for him to shake. Then, as was always her habit, she flipped his over for a little investigation. "Say—that's some palm. I'd like to browse around in that."

"Perhaps on some other occasion." Dooley discreetly withdrew his hand . . . Lord knows what she might have read in those lines.

"Hi there!" squawked Felix, who was riding on Dooley's shoulder.

"Hello, bird!" said Madame Sosostris. "Pollywanna-cracker?"

"No!" Felix plumed his feathers regally. "How about a dish of ectoplasm?"

"That's some bird, Tim. Where did—"

"Madame S., we're in kind of a hurry. May we look at Lorenzo's diary? Where we found the genie spell."

"Your books, lad. That never panned out, did it?"

"Well—uh—" I pretended to be very busy at those notebooks.

"It's important to differentiate between genuine occultism and silly fairy tales."

"Like genies, mistress?" Dooley had himself a little private joke.

"Here's the passage!" Nobody seemed to be taking this seriously—not even Dooley—except me. I thumbed through some pages and found what I wanted. "Listen! There's more. He went back to the British Museum." I explained to Dooley, "That's where he found the spell."

He was paying attention by now, all right. "May his scholarship be blessed!"

"I took out the page with the spell on it—but here's another entry from London. 'May 20, 1938. I continue to be entranced by Al-Hazred's *Necronomicon*. And have discovered a few more pages of it—though much mutilated. Apparently the Slave of the Carpet incurred the Wizard's wrath, for he writes, *On this, the last day of Ramadan in the seventh year of the reign of the Great Haroun Al-Raschid—' "*

Dooley shuddered—I'd never seen him frightened before—and murmured, "*Ayee!*—the fatal day—"

" '—*I have bound the sinner in his lower prison.* Then many lines obliterated—until this phrase—*and she above all!—the orchid of the guarded garden—!* Then three lines blurred, and—*in my bones I feel his mastery depart, as the mortal appetite possesses him.*' "

"What's mortal appetite?"

"Shh, Madame Sosostris." We were at the crux. I went on reading, " 'Much lost. And final entry *most* enigmatic! *Yet my own heart, mortal, despite my magic, does pity the poor potent fool. Therefore have I written the runes of his release—*' Would that be the spell, Dooley, do you think?"

"Read on!" Dooley urged. His eyes were burning—almost like in the tapestry.

" '—*and he shall be ever with them, and yet never see the words.*' I don't understand—"

"Read *on!*"

" '*And should I choose to summon him, and he defy my will once more, I can return him to the deadly delicate web again by one word only—*' "

Dooley started and said nervously, "One word—" It was really upsetting to see this—this being who I thought was so powerful, become so afraid.

I went on reading, " '—*for to seal the spell I have decreed that the mere pronouncing of the five letters printed upon the stars, which all the children of the Highest among men revere, shall fall upon his ears like thunder and resolve his soul among the threads.*' " It was as if a chill wind blew through the séance room after I'd spoken those cryptic words. "That's all there is." I sort of shivered. "But I'd like to know—what does it mean?"

Madame Sosostris just shrugged her shoulders—she didn't know what was happening anyway—but Dooley slowly and fatefully shook his head, as if he'd seen a black cloud beginning to gather in his west.

The bell over the front door tinkled, and Madame Sosostris went into the front room to see who'd come into the shop.

"Don't you understand *anything* of it, Dooley?" I asked.

"Bits, master." His cloud seemed to get darker. "But 'tis typical of the Wizard's nature that he hid his threats and promises in words of mystery."

"Listen, I have an idea. That man at the museum translated the spell that let you out of the carpet—let's go up and ask him."

"Very well," sighed Dooley. "But Al-Hazred took a malicious delight in concealing his secrets. I doubt that any mortal man can unravel them."

"It's worth a try."

We said goodbye to Madame Sosostris, who was trying

to sell a pair of medieval Spanish candlesticks—they were real, too—to a skeptical customer, and drove up to the National Museum.

In the car Dooley was very pensive and still. He put Felix on my shoulder and, when the parakeet began to talk, he said, "Bird, be silent! I'm in no mood for your ironies today."

The silence, as we drove uptown, got very oppressive. I had to say *something*—so I said, "I wonder what that business of 'the orchid of the guarded garden'—"

"Ah, that I can explain!" For a second a smile lightened his face. "Sofaya, loveliest of the Wizard's women! He kept her in a sequestered glade. It was she who caused my downfall, master. And, lo, she is dust these centuries ago."

"How did she cause your downfall, Dooley?"

"She lightly smote me with her eyes." He laughed, but at something sad, not funny. "And in that delicate blow was my defeat. Her beauty pained me, my heart trembled like a veil, my knees quaked like the sliding earth—and I felt love, the mortal passion, appetite, which the Wizard had forbidden me. He felt my sin against his might, and felt my magic dwindling, and in a rage confined me in the frightful carpet. 'For love,' he said, 'enchants enchanters.' "

It all came clear. "And that's what's happening right now! You're falling for Rose. Poor Sam. His ears are probably hanging down to his shoulders by now."

Dooley was still off in his reverie. "An orchid," he mused. "A rose. Ah, master, there is much beyond my magic. Much even beyond my imagining. I made a song of my sadness—"

"What about those letters 'printed upon the stars'?"

"I know not, master." He'd barely heard me and began to sing:

> *More potent than the sun am I*
> *And subtle as the air,*
> *But joy I find not on the earth*
> *Nor pleasure anywhere.*
>
> *For he who bound me in his spell*
> *Forbade me use my heart.*
> *A loveless life I live in vain,*
> *A creature made by art.*

There were several other stanzas, too. It was really a lovely song. I wish I could put down the melody, but I don't know music yet. It was even prettier than *"Plaisir d'amour"* . . . And it filled up the time till we got to the National.

I thought we'd have to leave Felix in the car, but Dooley said no, he'd get stolen or lonely or something. It was a chilly day for July, and I had a jacket on. Dooley pulled my pocket open with one hand and motioned inside with the other. "Compress thy feathers, little friend, and enter."

"Dark! Dark!" squealed Felix objectingly.

"I *said*—"

"Okay, okay." Felix knew it was no afternoon to cross the Genie. He tightened himself and crawled into my pocket. Where, in a muffled voice, he made one last complaint: "Big bully! Magic isn't everything."

"I'm well aware of that, bird," said Dooley softly. He wasn't at all like his usual self—a big bear or bull charged with mystery and power. Not that afternoon. "Come, master, let us seek the scholar's help."

We found Mr. Dickinson in the same crowded little cubicle where he had been before. I introduced Dooley, and Mr. Dickinson said eagerly, "Are you interested in Arabic studies, too?"

"*Extremely* interested!" the Genie said.

"Dooley, why don't you browse around the Near Eastern wing, while I go over these pages from Lorenzo's diary with Mr. Dickinson? Try to find out about those runes—and those letters printed upon the stars that will 'fall upon his ears like thunder—' "

Dooley flinched, as if he were about to be hit, and said, "An excellent suggestion."

"We have our famous Al-Hazred room," Mr. Dickinson offered brightly. "That's where the tapestry hangs that this young linguist was so interested in."

"I have seen much of it." Dooley smiled at me wanly. "And am like to see much more." He left.

I showed Mr. Dickinson the pages I'd brought up. "Fascinating! How fascinating!" he exclaimed, with that special enthusiasm that only a scholar can get when he finds a rare new document.

"I think 'the runes of his release' just mean the spell—"

"Very probably."

"This is the part I'm most interested in."

"Mmm. 'Printed upon the stars—' Five letters." He frowned at the pages, wanting them to give up their secrets. " 'Which all the children of the Highest among men revere.' Mmm." A thought was swimming in his head, somewhere down deep. "Well, now here at least I can be of help. This quotation from Al-Hazred purports to be of the time of the caliphate of Haroun Al-Raschid—is that not so?"

"Yes. It says so right here. The seventh year of his reign."

"It happened to be the custom in those days to refer to Mohammed the Prophet himself as 'the Highest among men.' "

"So all the children—"

"All the children of the 'Highest among men' would be all those people who are Mohammedan. Everyone who belongs to the religion of Islam. Well, of course—!" He smacked his forehead as that thought broke the surface. "Come here—I want to show you something."

In the back of his crazy little space—and you can't imagine how crowded it was!—there stood this great big pot, vase, whatever you want to call it. It was broken into about a million pieces, and you could see where Mr. Dickinson was laboriously gluing them back together again. "This," he said proudly, "is one of the very few stellar vases to survive from the period we were speaking of." He sniffed a bit. "My younger, more irreverent colleagues refer to it as 'Dickinson's star jar.' They were called stellar vases because, as you can see, even from the little bit left of this, the ornamentation on the surface represents the constellations. The Mohammedans believed—I wouldn't for a moment doubt it, although you can see pretty much what you want in the stars—they believed that the name of the Supreme Being whom they worshipped was written in the heavens in configurations of the stars." He traced a pattern, from star to star, on the vase. "You see? There, there—"

"What *is* that name?"

"In English, it would be A-L-L-A-H. The five letters printed upon the stars. Yes, indeed, in the minds of many Mohammedans, the greatest name in the world is Allah."

That was it then . . .

I thanked him, and without being too rude, I hoped, got out of there as quick as I could.

Dooley was in the tapestry room, staring up at himself. "Did you find the word, master?" he asked, without turning around to look at me.

"Yes."

"Am I like to hear it?"

"I don't think so."

"A single word." Now he smiled down at me and took my hand. "Verily, master, we tread upon the shells of eggs."

11

The Beginnings of a Birthday Party

An awful week of worry set in.

I did most of the worrying. Dooley got resigned pretty quick. He really expected the worst to happen. Here we'd gone down to Madame Sosostris's hoping to find a cure for the complications of his being a genie, and all we'd found out was that if he *did* fall in love with Rose, it was back to the rug. And in addition—to make matters worse—if he heard just one word, even accidentally, it was right back there just-like-that!

He explained it to me, though, Dooley did. He said that magic was like that—very unlike humanity. If two people have a quarrel, say, they can fume for days and then change their minds. You almost always get a second chance. But not with magic. It's very much stronger than human nature— but also much weaker, more vulnerable. Just one wrong word, or a sinister gesture, and a palace or a whole big city built by sorcery can zip into oblivion. Dooley said that that was the reason the Wizard forbade him to love. He said love was humanity's strongest point, and the thing that challenged magic most . . . I'm not sure I understand what he means, yet.

And poor Sam! We explained the situation to him, and if you ever saw anyone look dejected, you should have seen the face on this frightened basset-man. For a while he didn't say anything—just looked around the pet shop he loved. Then he made me promise, "If anything *does* happen, Timmy—I mean, if my dog gets too obvious—you *will* take care of the animals?"

"Sure, Sam." I did a stiff-upper-lip.

"Lucy's rich, and—"

"Sam!—I promise. Even if I have to sell Lorenzo's books."

It was awful! . . . It was one of those times like when someone is dying. And nobody's willing to admit a thing.

It also was awful for Dooley and Rose. He and I decided that the best thing would be if he didn't come to the apartment any more. Or at least as little as possible—only to pick up Aunt Lucy at the door when she had to be driven somewhere, and for *very* fast lunches. The rest of the time, in his own apartment, he'd concentrate on the spell, to keep Sam manly.

Rose was terribly hurt, but she wouldn't admit it. She hid it by saying in a newspaper voice, "Such a waste—such a criminal waste. With a voice like that." Because Dooley had stopped his singing, too, to stay away from her.

Rose was a special problem for me. All during that week I could think of nothing but one word—Allah—and how I could keep Dooley from hearing it. I told him to stay away from the United Nations, where there might be Near Eastern diplomats. And we had to give up going to Armenian restaurants. (He was teaching me to like all his favorite foods.) Then all of a sudden a danger point showed up right in the apartment.

It was those darn crossword puzzles of Rose. I came in to breakfast one morning, and before I could even say "scrambled," which is how I wanted my eggs that day, she went on to ask me, "And what's a potent Near Eastern deity, in five letters, Mr. Wisdom—from all you picked up in that shop in the Village?"

Well, I can tell you the thought of eggs instantly vanished from my mind! As it turned out, the name they wanted was Thoth, that Egyptian god they have the statue of up in the museum. But it set my mind to wondering. "Do those puzzles often ask questions like that, Rose?"

"All the time. I think the person who makes them up has a thing about religion. I get asked for the names of saints, Greek and Roman gods and goddesses, pre-Columbian somebody or other—it isn't fair." She began scrambling. "If your high-talkin' friend would do something more than just stick his face in here, he could probably help me with them a lot. With all the traveling he says he's done . . . The River Jordan—ha!"

So after that I had to get up very early every morning— the paper got delivered to the door—and go through the crossword puzzle bleary-eyed. Because I *hate* to get up early.

A really rotten week . . . But at least I couldn't think of any other way that Dooley could hear the Mohammedan word. At least New York has this advantage: everyone swears in Christian here.

It was rough on Aunt Lucy, too. More so than I knew at the time.

She took me aside one morning for one of those serious "grownup" talks that a grownup has with a kid when he knows that the kid won't like what he hears. It seems that the testing psychologist, with Mr. Watkins's enthusiastic support, had come to the conclusion that I *was* an antisocial child, about as well adjusted as a polar bear in Central

Africa, and I *did* need to go to summer camp—for all of August. Of course I objected violently. But only because the spell was hanging by a thread, and heaven knew what might happen in my absence. However, Aunt Lucy, with that chipmunk mind of hers, interpreted my resistance as absolute proof that the psychologist and Mr. Watkins were right. And they weren't! They were both dead wrong. You may not believe it, but I like the company of kids my own age. If they're interesting and fun, that is. Like Jimmy and Irving.

I asked Aunt Lucy if I could postpone it until next year—or shorten it to two weeks at least . . . No! No! No! . . . There was nothing to do but give in gracefully—and hope for the best.

But then, after the grownup part was through, our conversation got interesting. Aunt Lucy began to pick my brains about Sam. I still don't know if she knew what she was doing, but that little animal inside her, which had lately begun to spruce up, was feeling lonely and uncertain.

"How's the pet shop going?" she nonchalantly asked.

"Oh, fine."

"Sam seems to be very busy these days."

"He is." He'd been avoiding her. We had a talk about it, and Sam decided that if Dooley did lose control completely and Sam reverted to being a dog, he didn't want it to happen in front of Aunt Lucy. It would have upset her terribly.

"I've stopped by a couple of times—just on the way

home—" she did that thing of being indifferent, which women often do when they're not—"and he's always so preoccupied. The rabbits need water, or the puppies new paper."

"It's a hard job—" I tried to cover Sam's tracks—"running a pet shop all by yourself."

"I thought that we were becoming good friends." Of course she was dying to dig for information, but being ladylike, as well as little and pretty uncertain, she didn't know how. "Has Sam ever said— I mean, do you think I've done anything to offend him?"

"No, Aunt Lucy. Sam really likes you very much. It's just that—" It was just that the magic might collapse and Sam turn into a mutt again—and how do you explain all that to a maiden lady who lives in Sutton Place? —"It's just, he has problems, that's all."

"Oh, well." She shrugged it all off: unimportant. And then exclaimed, "But I have a marvelous idea!"—as if she'd just had a marvelous idea, when obviously she'd been hatching it for days. "Next week is your birthday—"

"How did you know that?"

"Oh, I know all about you, young man!" Ha! She'd checked with Madame Sosostris, I found out later. "And a few days later you'll be going to camp—so why don't we have a splendiferous birthday party for you? You might even pry Mr. Bassinger away from his pet shop—for one evening at least."

I think it was right then that I really began to like Aunt Lucy. She *did* want to give me a birthday party and make the grim going away to camp a little bit easier—but she also had doped out a way to get Sam back in the apartment again . . . I don't mind people being sneaky—if it's in a good cause, at least.

"Aunt Lucy," I said, "I would *love* that!"

But she didn't like the guest list much. There were no "little friends" on it. (Jimmy and Irving didn't know any of these new people in my life, so why invite them? They'd only be edgy.) I asked Madame Sosostris, Felix, Dooley, Rose, Sam, and of course Aunt Lucy. And that was all. It was plenty, too. They were all people I wanted to celebrate my birthday with. But Aunt Lucy invited Mr. Watkins. Or, to do her justice, he invited himself. On the afternoon of the party, just before it was supposed to start, he called up and said that he had some literature on the camp I was going to—naturally he'd advised her on its selection—would it be all right if he came around? From the telephone Aunt Lucy's expression asked me if he could.

She looked so hopeful, I nodded. My instinct said no, but my head nodded yes . . . It's a big mistake to distrust your instinct.

So everybody arrived. With presents. And presents are hard for teenagers—I was turning thirteen—because when you're a little kid, you can get toys and not too important things, but when you get up into your teens, people have to begin to make thinking decisions.

I'm sure Mr. Watkins had been clued in, because along with the stuff about Camp Jefferson, he gave me a transistor radio. I liked him then—and not just because of the radio, but for the way he gave it—"I thought this might be, well, fun at camp"—as if he was a little scared I wouldn't want to accept his present, and he *did* want to be part of my party . . . I guess that kitten I adopted at the shop has been teaching me to like cat people, without my knowing it.

Rose and Dooley collaborated on their present—but only over the telephone. Amid all the things that Aunt Lucy had bought for me, before I moved up, she'd forgotten a hi-fi set. So Dooley got me that—with his own earned money, he assured me, not magicked—and Rose got me all her favorite records. She said that she always got people presents that *she* liked, because that way at least she was sure of herself . . . It was a great selection, too—all the way from opera through pop to rock.

Madame Sosostris was a bit of a disappointment. I'd been sending thought waves down to Greenwich Village about that antique bull's-eye mirror, but she showed up with a miniature Eskimo totem pole. At first I was worried and thought I'd better whip it up into my closet with the rest of my weirdo stuff, but Aunt Lucy examined it with a great deal of interest. She was really coming along. For a while.

Her own gift was the biggest surprise of all: a beautiful set of prints of hunting dogs—really knockout drawings. "They're wonderful! Thank you," I said. "Look, Sam—"

Sam looked and mumbled something about how nice—but he got pretty fidgety and self-conscious.

Felix picked that up right away, of course. He eyed Sam, cackled his laugh, and asked, "Recognize anyone there, Fido?"

Dooley and I frowned seriously, and Felix shrieked an apology. He began to sing "Happy Birthday."

Felix was really the life of the party. He was standing on the topmost rung of his new platform—that was Sam's gift to me, by the way—and was he ever pleased with it! It had different levels, arranged in a spiral and all connected by elegant little curving ladders, on which my parakeet marched proudly up and down, cracking jokes and singing and having a marvelous time. I offered to set the stand up in my bedroom, but Aunt Lucy said—another good sign—that it was too beautiful, it belonged in the living room. So there it stood, with newspapers placed all around beneath it.

We were going to have a dinner party, called for sixish, and I wanted us all to have drinks before. Lorenzo had said that was very civilized—if it didn't go too far. There was water for Felix, in a cup hung on a special hook right under the topmost platform, and ginger ale for me, and whatever anyone else might want from Aunt Lucy's well-stocked bar.

I think that Aunt Lucy and Mr. Watkins were a little bit nervous at first, about having her servants as part of the party. But fortunately Dooley and Rose were not. And, being guests, they were *not* wearing uniforms. He'd bought a new suit, which was almost purple—but Dooley could get away with it—and a ruffled shirt, and Rose looked (not quite, but very close) more stylish than Aunt Lucy. She was wearing a slack suit and obviously enjoyed the pants flapping around her legs . . . I like it when some people show themselves off. If they do it the right way.

Although Dooley and Rose were guests, they were also very helpful. When it came time for canapés, they unobtrusively disappeared, and in a minute there was Dooley, passing a tray around.

He was also, less luckily, making drinks . . .

Sam had been a man now for a very short time. He should have been in his thirties—by dog chronology, that is—and he looked in his thirties, but as far as holding his liquor went, he was probably a few years behind me. And I've never had anything but half-glasses of wine, on birthdays down at the antique shop.

Mr. Watkins did a big-buddy thing: sidled up to Sam, put his arm around Sam's shoulder, trying to be friends with everyone, and said, "How about a martini, Bassinger?"

But a cat wanting to be friends makes a dog uneasy.

Sam twisted out from under Mr. Watkins's arm and said, "Oh—okay." That was the first of Sam's martinis.

The first of many . . . Now there are some things, like ice cream and steak, that dogs and people can enjoy together—but not booze! . . . I watched Mr. Watkins and Sam stroll off to the bar with a certain amount of apprehension.

I would have gone after them, to make a little margin between them, but Rose came up just then and said, "Hey, Mr. Birthday Boy!—you're not the only one who gets presents today."

"Who else, Rose?" I asked, with my eye on Sam.

"Me!" she boasted. "Look! A gift from our long-lost and elusive friend Dooley. He knows my passion." She gave me a paperback book with the title *A Selection of Best Crossword Puzzles,* and subtitled—as if that wasn't bad enough!—"gathered from English-language newspapers throughout the globe."

That was just what I needed. I thought of the weeks that I'd be away, and Rose now having a grand excuse to call Dooley up and ask him questions . . . The poor guy— he'd probably say the word, in all innocence, and kayo himself back into the carpet before he even knew what hit him.

"That's very nice, Rose. May I look through it?"

"Sure, help yourself. I'm putting on the beef—" For beef Stroganoff, a favorite of mine—I'd requested it. "The madame shouldn't be too long with her tricks, should she?"

"Half an hour at most, Rose."

"Okay." She went into the kitchen.

I hid the book between the cushions of the couch. Tomorrow I was going to slip it down the incinerator, behind Rose's back. And then have to lie about having forgotten where I had placed it.

Madame Sosostris, when I had invited her to my party, proclaimed that as a special favor she would do her magic tricks. And if Madame Sosostris was a success as an antique dealer, and a moderate success as a medium—at least trying hard—she was a *disaster* as a magician! All she knew were the old corny things like disappearing coins and handkerchiefs being pulled through rings and old-fashioned junk like that. But when I told Dooley we were going to have to sit through all her parlor tricks, he shined on me with one of his smiles and said, "Master, shall we also make *this* a special occasion for our struggling Occult Scientist?"

You can bet I said yes . . . So this was one magic show I was really looking forward to.

High time for it, too. On the other side of the living room Mr. Watkins and Sam had gotten into a heated conversation. In fact Sam, who was belting another martini, looked quite hot under the collar. Aunt Lucy, who had been checking with Rose about the Stroganoff, was casting anxious glances toward them.

I interrupted everything by marching out living-room center and announcing, "Ladies and gentlemen—and parakeet—Madame Sosostris has kindly consented to entertain us with a few magic tricks before dinner. Madame S.—go into your act."

The humans applauded, and Felix squawked enthusiastically.

Madame Sosostris bowed and said, "For my first endeavor—"

Her first endeavor was usually the disappearing coin, a Spanish doubloon, in this case. It was twiddled around in her fingers a minute, and then, when the back of her hand was turned, down the sleeve of her blouse. And was it ever obvious—wow! Even Felix turned to me with as much of a skeptical expression as a parakeet can have and said mockingly, "*Aw haw!*"

Dooley and I had decided to let that one get by and start in on her with the second endeavor.

We all applauded for politeness' sake. Except Mr. Watkins. Perhaps he thought it was funny or clever, but he purred silkily, "Delightful, Madame Sosostris, delightful. But would you dare to untuck your blouse just now?"

There was that awful embarrassed pause when someone you like is exposed as a fake.

"Sharp eyes, Mr. Watkins," said Madame Sosostris. "For my second endeavor—" across the room Dooley gave me a colossal wink—"I shall produce—*from the empty air*—a series of the most delicate silk scarves."

The series of scarves was produced from an enormous hollow gold bracelet she wore on her left wrist. The idea was to make it look as if they all were coming from the palm of her hand. There were five of them: red, blue, green, gold, purple—and each new one elicited an "oh" or an "ah," from Madame Sosostris, if not from her audience. At the purple, the last, she did a big thing of flourishing the raggedy string in the air.

But this time, as she began her flourish, the purple was *not* the last. A gorgeous piece of silk appeared, with all different dazzling colors mixed into it . . . And now there was a real "oh" from the audience.

"That's *lovely*!" Rose exclaimed.

"Yeah, isn't it?" said Madame Sosostris nervously.

Nobody was watching him except me, but I could see Dooley doing little things with his fingers. Mixing colors, I suspect.

The next scarf to appear was even more brilliant than the first had been. I'm not going to try to describe the scarves. There aren't that many words for colors in the whole English language. And if there were, I wouldn't know half of them.

More beautiful even than the scarves was Madame Sosostris's face—the changing expressions there. At first she just couldn't believe her eyes and kept unrolling them like paper towels. But then, finally, she trusted what was happening. Her face flushed even more happily with each of the scarves she pulled out. It was just like down at the antique shop, with the Willy sisters—she was sure she was having a breakthrough.

Now she really became a magician—grandly unreeling scarf after scarf. Until it was my turn to wink at Dooley. Because enough is enough. Even of fun. Besides, I was hungry. I could smell the Stroganoff . . . And we still had the egg to go through.

Madame Sosostris's third endeavor was a hard-boiled egg inside her turban. She would reach behind, as if patting her hair down, and magically produce the egg. I hoped it would work. There was one time, down in the Village, when she accidentally bumped her turban, coming into the séance room, and then gracefully called off the trick, excused herself, and went into the kitchen, where, when she got her turban off, her hair was all covered with bits of hard-boiled white and yolk.

Well, she lifted her hand up with a very grandiose, lengthy gesture—and just as she was about to extract the egg, her head suddenly drooped beneath an unexpected weight. She barely got the thing out in time, before it sprained her neck. And it was an egg, all right—but a huge egg, made of marble, so big that it filled her whole hand, like those sculptured eggs that come from Florence, Italy.

By now Madame S. was absolutely convinced that the Spirits were helping her out with her act. She reached around and patted her turban, to find what else might be there, pretending she was primping. I'd never seen Madame S. primping before, and as far as I was concerned, that was by far the best part of the show. She's always been kind of a horsy woman and really doesn't know how to primp; patting herself all around like that, she looked as if she were posing for old-fashioned movie stills.

But the egg was all. Dooley called off his magic, Madame Sosostris at last gave up, and we went in to eat.

Aunt Lucy had ordered the works: the table all decorated with Grampa Lorenzo's oldest china, candelabra, and everything. I never thought she'd let me do it, but she even allowed me to bring in Felix. I perched him on one of the branches of a candelabrum, and he spent the whole meal yodeling and cracking jokes and repeating, "Wow! What a spread! It sure beats birdseed." (He got that last from me. Because when I put him on the silver limb, I asked him if this didn't beat birdseed.)

We were all in very high spirits, because of Felix and Madame Sosostris's unexpected success. After getting over the shock of seeing her chauffeur and her cook sitting down at her dining-room table, Aunt Lucy enjoyed herself, too. All except Sam, that is. He was sitting on the opposite side of the table from me, fuming and woofing to himself about something.

We didn't find out what it was until the time for dessert came around: baked Alaska, the climax of the meal—but it was spoiled by a fight beginning. "Timmy—" Sam burst out—he'd had wine with dinner too—"is it true that they're shipping you off to camp?"

"Yes, Sam." I hadn't told him, wanting to break it to him gently, in private. "But only for a few weeks."

"Well, what am *I* supposed to do?"

"What's the matter, Bassinger?" Mr. Watkins purred. "Can't you tend your pet shop without the little chappy's help?"

"No!" I could see Sam's hackles beginning to rise. "We've never been separated—not since that day I was found—"

"Shall we have coffee in the living room?" Aunt Lucy's Sutton Place instinct knew just when to interrupt.

We all murmured our relieved agreement.

But it didn't do any good . . . This quarrel had been in the cards, or the fur, ever since the two of them had met.

"But why *camp*—?"

"Cognac, Sam?" said Aunt Lucy, still doing her best.

"Sure." Sam swigged down a snifter of brandy. "He won't know any of the other kids—"

"I don't mind, Sam—really. I think I'd like—"

"That's exactly the point." Mr. Watkins now became logical, which for some reason that I don't understand made him behave as if I wasn't even there. "Dr. Friedlinger said the boy was well on the way to becoming a regular little eccentric. He needs the companionship of his peer group, and Lucy and I—"

"Yes, and you, Lucy!" Sam glared at her balefully. "I don't understand how *you* could do this—if you love him."

"Of course I love him—"

I didn't quite understand how a "little eccentric"—me—could also be "regular," but no matter. The whole point now was to stop the fight. *"Honestly,* Sam—I don't mind—"

"Well, I do!" said Sam. "And it makes me angry!"

"Mad dog! Mad dog!" screamed Felix, to enrich the confusion.

Aunt Lucy was pouring coffee like crazy, and Dooley and Rose were sitting side by side on the couch, with that embarrassed I-wish-I-wasn't-here look of people who have to watch their employers quarrel in public . . . It was getting to the point where I would even have welcomed a few more lousy magic tricks.

By now Mr. Watkins had his own hackles up. If cats have hackles. He kind of spat out, "As long as we're on the subject, Lucy—and this is something the little chappy should know—" Thanks a lot! As if I hadn't heard everything already. "I've been thinking about his schooling. September's only a month away—"

A feeling of dread got hold of me. "Public school will be fine," I said hopefully.

"—and I've taken the liberty of getting in touch with the

headmaster of the General Ulysses S. Grant Military Academy."

"Military Academy!" Sam stood up and tried to steady himself.

"It's a very fine boarding school." Mr. Watkins stood up, too. "My alma mater. And I'm proud of it, if I may say so. By the way, Bassinger," he added sneakily, "what's *your* school?"

"Life, Henry!" Sam snarled. "I picked up my education in the streets. And why don't you just keep your cold nose out of Timmy's business anyway?"

"Dooley!" Aunt Lucy squeaked desperately. "We're out of coffee—"

We weren't, but Dooley took the pot, said, "Yes, mistress," and bumped Sam purposefully on his way to the kitchen.

"Boarding school. And military school. The General Ulysses S. Grant Military Academy!" The bump had done no good at all. "That means he'll be away all the time—"

It went too fast now. I stood up myself. "Sam—!"

"You quiet schemer, you! You just want to turn him into a little cookie-cutter person. All stamped out like everyone else." And with that, I am sorry to say, Sam punched Mr. Watkins in the eye.

"Sam, *stop!*" Aunt Lucy was on her feet now, too. We all were, milling around like animals, not knowing what to do.

"You've had too much to drink—" I said.

"I can hold my liquor," Sam announced, in a voice as unsteady as his legs. "Remember the time Lorenzo spilled the whole bottle of beer in my pan and—" His face changed abruptly. "I feel sick," he admitted and lurched into the hall toward the john.

"It's a proud school," said Mr. Watkins defensively. He was feeling around the puffy edges of what was surely going to be a black eye. "With a great name. Indeed, in the minds of many military historians, the greatest name in the world—"

The door from the kitchen swung in—Dooley coming back with the coffee pot.

And from nowhere—dry space—a voice squawked, "Yes, indeed, in the minds of many Mohammedans, the greatest name in the world is Allah."

12

And the Birthday Party's End

Felix! . . . With that memory of his.

So many things happened all at once.

By luck I was the only one who'd been looking at Dooley. Or rather looking where Dooley had been. The coffee pot hung suspended a second—just floating in empty air—then crashed to the floor. Now all eyes turned to the mess of broken china and coffee spreading along the living-room rug.

But all ears went into the hall, where a wild barking had begun. Sam stumbled in, tottering, and collapsed—collapsed on all four legs. And if you think that a dog can't look panic-stricken, just as much as a man, then you should have seen his eyes.

"Timothy!" Aunt Lucy couldn't believe her *own* eyes. "Have you been concealing that dog?"

I was—flummoxed, dumfounded, speechless.

"Timothy—I want an answer! Has that dog been hidden in this apartment all this time?"

"Well—he's been here part of the time—but—"

"Oh, Timothy—" She did a big betrayed routine, eyes lifting away from me, as if I were something that had just got broken—"I thought we were friends—that we both could be honest—"

"Aunt Lucy, we *can*, but—!"

Mr. Watkins looked down contemptuously at Sam, who was flattened out on the floor and whimpering pathetically. "I thought that mutt got gassed."

"He looks pretty gassed to me," Rose observed.

"Rose, *where* in this apartment—?"

"Miss Lucy—" Rose had a tone of voice that no one dared doubt—"I haven't seen a hair of him."

"And *where* is Dooley? Did he just—*throw* the coffee pot at me?"

Sam had recycled, back into a hound dog; Abdullah was

trapped in his carpet again; and Aunt Lucy, too, was reverting into a short snobby lady, indignant over the loss of a china coffee pot in her posh apartment in Sutton Place.

"Let me have a look." Rose went into the kitchen.

"Um—I guess the party's breaking up." Breaking up— it had been smashed into smithereens! But Madame Sosostris went on doing the best she could to fill up a silence when nobody else would talk. "Delicious dinner, Miss Farr—"

"So *pleased* you could come." Aunt Lucy thinned out a smile at her.

"Miss Lucy—" Rose came back—"he's gone."

"Gone?"

"Vanished." She was pretending to be only reporting the latest information, but her voice was hurt as well as puzzled.

Aunt Lucy sighed and brushed her forehead with weary fingertips. "There must be some disease peculiar to my chauffeurs." Another confusion occurred to her. "And speaking of disappearing—where's Sam?"

"He's gone home!" I blurted, before anybody could guess or suspect. "I think."

"And well he might! Behaving that way. Poor Henry—"

"I knew the chap was vicious the first day I laid eyes on him," said Mr. Watkins, who by now had a genuine shiner blossoming on his face.

"Rose, did you cook all the beef?"

" 'Fraid so, Miss Lucy. And I don't think a slice of stroganoff would help that eye any."

"This is *not* a time for levity."

"Sorry, Miss Lucy . . ." But thank heaven someone still had a sense of humor.

We shuffled a little more in our talk, and then Madame Sosostris and Mr. Watkins went home.

"Just clean up as best you can for tonight," Aunt Lucy said to Rose. She retired to her bedroom, with all kinds of exasperated sounds. "I've had as much as I can take for one day."

So had I!

I collected Sam from the living-room rug and carried him into our bedroom. At first I thought I'd get the spell and pull everything back together again. But then I decided there already was so much chaos around, if everybody reappeared, it would only make things worse. One night in the carpet wouldn't be too bad for Dooley, and one night in his box wouldn't be too bad for Sam. In fact, he deserved it. I poured him out on his cushion, which I'd kept there for old times' sake, and said, "Now just go to sleep," and thought that was the end of my birthday party . . . It wasn't.

The next end was, while I was dozing off, I heard Sam stir and pad into the hall, still weaving a little, toward

Aunt Lucy's room. I followed him. Her door was ajar, and he nosed it open and stood there, just looking.

She'd changed into pajamas and was sitting at her dressing table, wearing a housecoat with butterflies on it. She saw Sam watching. At first she was angry: her little features frowned, remembering all the broken bottles, I guess. But then, in spite of themselves, they relaxed. She patted her knee and said, "Come in, Sam."

Sam approached her very carefully.

"Good old Sam," she said. "I'm almost glad to see you again."

Sam lifted one paw to her knee. Which she shook. And then ordered him gently, "Go on, now. Go back to Timmy's room."

He came into the hall—and found me watching. His head drooped down, ashamed . . . So did mine. I don't like to eavesdrop. Even on dogs.

The next morning Sam was sure he was dying. He lay in his box making fatal sounds—low howls, whinings, and sighs of doggy despair—which I have to admit I thought were quite funny.

"Sam, it *isn't* hydrophobia." I tried to console him. "It's only a hangover."

With a little coaxing, he lapped up two aspirins from the palm of my hand. But you know how dogs are about pills.

Even after some water they got stuck in his throat. He didn't like the taste of them either and made me an angry face and gave a very disgruntled woof.

Then I thought an ice pack might help, so I got some ice cubes out of the freezer and tied them up in my face cloth. But the string came untied, and the ice fell all over his head.

Poor Sam . . . I was being mean, and laughing and having fun at his expense . . . The best thing was just to let him sleep it off.

At breakfast Rose was preoccupied. She hadn't even asked me what I wanted the ice cubes for. I suspected her mood was because of Dooley— little wise guy that I was that day, but I was going to get what was coming to me— and I asked her, all fake innocence, if she'd heard from him yet this morning.

"No." She stirred her coffee and made the cup rattle. "And we probably won't."

"Why not, Rose?"

"I think he's just one of those rolling stones, that's all. You heard him tell about all those places he's been— swimming in the River Jordan. Probably in some place like Bangladesh right now!" She sipped her coffee, spilled some on her chin, and said, "Damn!"

"I wouldn't be surprised if Dooley came back, Rose." Little Mr. Fixit here—all I had to do was recite the spell.

"Well, *I* would!"

"You sort of liked him, didn't you, Rose?"

"Oh, sure." She could do some faking, too. "He was okay, I guess."

"You liked him quite a lot—"

"Just finish your breakfast, nosey. And leave the psychologizing to Freud. You got troubles of your own! With that dog."

But the funny thing was, I didn't. At least not the troubles Rose was thinking of.

Aunt Lucy came into the kitchen, and before anybody could even offer "good morning," she formally announced, "Timothy, I've decided that you can keep Sam."

"I can *keep* him—?" Complications swarmed like bees in my head.

"Yes, dear. If you love him enough to have hidden him all this time—although I can't imagine where. Probably right under our noses, Rose— Well, it's cruel to want someone so much and then have him suddenly—"

"I'll have to ask Sam—" I was thinking out loud.

"*Ask* Sam?"

"I mean—tell him. He'll be happy. To be out in the open. At least, I think he will—"

She attributed my confusion to childish pleasure and surprise, and gave me a very auntlike smile. "You tell him then. And tell him that all is forgiven between us."

"Between you and Sam? He'll be glad to hear that."

Aunt Lucy chuckled to Rose at my charming belief that Sam could understand what I said. But I was sure hoping he could—that enough of his understanding had lasted—because it was going to have to be his decision. Aunt Lucy was going out for the morning, and I left her and Rose in the kitchen, discussing what to have for lunch.

Sam was snoring in his box. "Wake up, Sam." He likes to have me wake him up by scratching his neck.

"Woof," he said sleepily. He still was bleary-eyed, but seemed much better than when I had left him.

"Aunt Lucy says I can keep you."

"Woof?"

"I mean—keep you as a dog."

"*Woof!*" He jumped out of his box. And he was understanding, all right. "*Woofwoofwoofwoofwoof!*"

"All right, all right, Sam. Cool it now." There's such a difference between a yes woof and a no. "But you acted very badly last night. You acted—like a dog."

"Woof," he apologized and hung his head.

"You might be happier—"

"*Woof!*"

"It's hard being a man. You may not be up to it—"

"Woof!" he declared.

"—and I'd love you just as much—"

"Woof. Woooooooof—" he pleaded and laid his head on top of my foot.

"Well, all right. But this is your last chance. I'll get the spell. I've got to get Dooley out of the carpet anyway."

I pulled a chair over in front of the closet, to reach the top compartment. I was wondering if I could say it right there and Dooley would just appear in my bedroom—or whether a better idea would be to go back to—

The top shelf was empty . . . No bone, no Aztec bowl, not any of my special things. And no Good-Luck Devil from Borneo.

"It's gone—" I said, but couldn't believe.

Sam started barking hysterically. No conversational woofing now—just pure canine panic at the thought that he might be trapped in himself for the rest of his life.

"Hush up, Sam!" I tried to put a plug in the volcano of fright that was erupting in my chest, too. "Rose may have only moved things around—"

But in the kitchen she shot down any hope I had. "That junk in the closet?"

"Yes, Rose. That junk."

"You remember the day, a month or so ago, when you stayed out so late at night?"

"Yes—"

"Well, next morning, when you were gone, your aunt said there were going to be some changes made around here. And the first one was, I should throw out all those creepy things you lugged up from the Village."

"Did you—?"

"Right down the incinerator."

"But the statuette—with the hollow eyes—"

"That little old ugly idol?—it went down first of all."

"Oh, my gosh!"

"What's wrong with that animal?"

"Easy, Sam." I tried to soothe him and stroked his head. "I have to think."

All I could think of to do was go back to Lorenzo's diaries. (I looked through the last couple of pages I'd taken from them. Instead of putting them in the closet, I'd just tucked them in my copy of *The Hobbit*. Save time, I thought.)

In the cab Sam was whining pitifully. The driver, who was a nice man, thought I was taking him to the veterinarian and kindly asked, "What's wrong with your pooch?"

"Mister," I said, "if I even tried to tell you, you'd take us both straight to the psycho ward at Bellevue."

I kept petting Sam's head, although it felt funny—knowing it had been a man's head only yesterday.

We barged into the shop, which luckily was empty except for Madame S. But every browser in Greenwich Village couldn't have stopped Sam or me that day. "Madame Sosostris, we've *got* to find—"

"Hi, Tim. And *Sam*—!"

"—that genie spell again!"

"When did Sam get back?"

"Never *mind*! Please help me, Madame S. You don't know how important this is—"

"I don't see why." She shrugged. "That spell's a bust."

"No, it's *not*!" There was nothing else to do. To help me she'd have to know the truth. "You know Dooley—?"

"Sure. Your aunt's—"

"He's a genie," I said as factually as I could.

"And he moonlights as a chauffeur on the side?" She treated herself to a little chuckle.

"Don't *joke*! This is critical. That's how I smuggled him into the house. He came from a rug that's up in the National Museum, and he got returned there last night—by that one word 'Allah'—and it's horrible for him. Because he's already been in there a thousand years. But it's even worse for Sam. I mean, Mr. Bassinger—"

"Mr. Bassinger?"

"Yes. Mr. Bassinger is Sam. That is—Sam is Mr. Bassinger. I mean—they were going to exterminate Sam, so my genie turned him into a man, and—"

"Timothy—" Madame Sosostris put her hand on my shoulder—"I'm going to fix you an Alka-Seltzer with some soothing nightshade—"

"Oh, I *knew* nobody would ever believe me!" I had to find some proof—and I did. "Madame Sosostris, you remember your last séance with the Willy sisters?"

"The best I ever—"

"Dooley did that. The Fiendish Laughter—impersonating Nelly Willy—everything. Has anything like that happened since?"

She thought for a minute and admitted, "No—"

"I don't mean to put you down, Madame S.—sooner or later I'm certain you'll have your breakthrough—but it was Dooley who did all that. And last night—the bracelet trick, with all those extra scarves. And since when have you been able to carry a marble egg as big as a dinosaur's inside that turban of yours?"

The beautiful thing about Madame Sosostris is how quickly she believes.

One minute more and she held out her hand. "Put 'er there." We shook. "To conjure a genie—wow!"

"So you see that we've got to find that spell."

She rolled up the sleeves of her blouse. "Let's go!"

And we ransacked those books like bandits . . .

But nothing . . . Absolutely nothing . . . No way . . . Lorenzo had left England a few days after the last entry about Al-Hazred. And he hadn't gone back to the British Museum again . . . Oh, why hadn't I made a copy? . . .

"We're licked," I admitted into a silence that was crushing us like iron.

Sam was lying on the floor, crying. He *was crying*, too, although most dogs don't cry—their eyes just water to wash out the junk. A last bit of Sam's humanity left over, I suppose. As his smile had been its beginning.

"What a way to celebrate your thirteenth birthday."

Madame Sosostris sighed. "But then, it's always been an evil number."

"I should have stayed twelve forever," I said.

My birthday party was *really* over now.

13

The National Museum

"There's only one thing left," I decided. "We have to go up to the National and talk to Mr. Dickinson. Naturally he'll think it's all nonsense, but maybe he's got a good memory. In Arabic." Better than me, I hoped. I couldn't even remember the spell in English. "And if that doesn't work, I'll tell Aunt Lucy that unless she flies me to England, I'll jump off the Brooklyn Bridge."

So into a taxi, the three of us . . . Up to the museum

. . . I deposited Sam in the bushes again, the way I had last time. He fretted and woofed a grumble at me, because of being left behind on such an important occasion, but I got him settled at last.

And down to Mr. Dickinson's office. "Now play it real cool, Madame S.," I said. "This guy is a scholarly type, and I'll tell him—I'll tell him you're doing research on incantations—okay?"

"Okay," she whispered, enjoying the conspiracy.

"Well, *hello!*" He recognized me right away. And seemed quite glad to see us, after all that broken crockery.

I made the introductions.

"Oh—incantations. Most interesting," Mr. Dickinson allowed.

"Yeah. I'm a medium," said Madame Sosostris. "I need all the spells I can get."

His eyes began to quiz her dubiously, so I barged right in to the point. "Mr. Dickinson—that genie spell I brought in —do you happen to remember it?"

"Oh dear no! I have the worst memory in the world." Great! "I have to leave myself a note to close the window." Mr. Dickinson's hair was a very strange thing. It was as if, when he got an idea, it tingled in those white puff balls on top of his ears. "But wait a minute. Was there something about a 'lunar eye'?"

"Yes! yes! That comes back. What else—"

"Um-uh-er—" He rummaged through his mind, which

was full of pieces of crockery. Then he shrugged and said, "I'm afraid that's all I can recollect."

"Oh, Lord, Mr. Dickinson—!"

"Where is this carpet anyway?" said Madame Sosostris.

"Upstairs. You've never seen it?"

"No."

"Would you like to?"

"Yes."

"Mr. Dickinson, *please*! We've got to—"

"Now, now, my boy. Don't exercise yourself so." He made an aside to Madame Sosostris: "Marvelous imagination, the lad has!"

"Imagination, eh?" murmured Madame S.

Then he included me: "It can't hurt just to look at the Wizard's tapestry."

But it did.

There was Dooley. I knew he was in there instantly— through his eyes. But they weren't burning now, with rage or hatred or anything—they were pleading. Almost as sad as Sam's . . . I couldn't bear to look at them . . . And the room was full of gawking museumgoers, all staring up at poor Dooley and not even dreaming what they were seeing.

But Madame Sosostris knew. If she'd had any lingering doubts, they were gone by now. She recognized his face and shot me a wild excited look.

"Do you like it, Madame Sosostris?" asked Mr. Dickinson.

"It's *unbelievable*!"

No teacher can keep from doing his thing when he's got a willing audience. "The filagreed border is of special interest. It's quite unlike any other of the period."

"How?"

"Mr. Dickinson—" I was wringing out my brains like a dishcloth—"wasn't 'skin of night' part of it, too?"

"Well, the elaboration of the floral motifs is so complex." Absolutely ignored, I was, in his scholarly enthusiasm. "That leafy pattern unfolding along the top border, for instance—" He stopped.

"Yes? . . . Yes?" said Madame Sosostris.

But there are some silences you shouldn't interrupt. I took her hand and squeezed it: quiet!

He made thinking noises. "Mmm. Hmm! Hmm-*hmm*!"

At last I couldn't stand any more. "Mr. Dickinson—?"

"It's really quite extraordinary."

Through my heart there blew a little breeze of hope. "What's—extraordinary, Mr. Dickinson?"

"You see that green vine—with the red vine running in back of it—?"

"Yes—"

"It's been twisted to such a degree that it almost looks like Arabic script."

"Oh, boy—"

"It isn't really my field of research—"

"Mr. Dickinson, *please*!"

"Yes, there *are* some letters interwoven into it. Mmmm-mmm—it's the esoteric priestly language of the time of Haroun Al-Raschid. Even then it was almost obsolete."

"Does it say anything?"

"Mm—'Genie, formed of earth and sky—' "

"That's the spell! The runes of his release." In the carpet Dooley's eyes changed, too, just like the quickening in my chest. They got bright as lightning. "Read the rest."

"I can't make it out—this is really amazing!—there's a shadow on that side. Here, just a minute—" Nobody gets more worked up than a scholar on top of a big discovery. Mr. Dickinson herded everybody else from the room. "Sorry—beg pardon—this room is closed. So sorry—get along there, will you, please—we have some repairs to make." When he'd pushed all the people out, he got a ROOM CLOSED sign from a corner and put it on the door. "Now help me take it down."

"Take it down?" This *was* the National, after all.

"Yes, *down*!" Madame S. and I helped him lower the carpet to the floor. "This will *make* my reputation." He took off his shoes and began to crawl around the border, peering down at that green vine. "Such a thrilling surprise!"

"You're in for an even bigger one, brother!" Madame Sosostris got the feel of the magic, too, whipped off her sneakers, and started to pad around herself.

" 'Genie—' " he made it out slowly, with difficulty—

" 'formed of earth and sky/skin of night, with lunar eye—' "

"Hold it!" I said. An all-too-familiar voice, desperately calling me, barked up from the floor below. "Don't say any more. And don't translate it. I'll be right back." I dashed out of the room and downstairs.

Sam hadn't been able to stand it in the bushes one minute more. He'd followed a bunch of people up the museum steps and, mixing himself in their legs, had seen his chance and charged into the huge front hall.

"Dog!"—"Dog!"—"Hey! Stop that dog!"—"There's a dog in here!"

The museum guards were in the biggest tizzy they'd enjoyed in years. Poor Sam—you'd have thought he was a mad vandal with a hammer. But with all those statues standing around, and the breakable vases, a dog in a museum is just about as welcome as the bull in the china shop.

As I came down the stairs, the uproar was on my left: the Roman rooms. The guards were all bumping into each other, shouting, "Where is he?"—"Where's that dog?"— and the ordinary museumgoers were milling around, having fun at it all, and making it hard for the guards—thank heaven!

Something told me that Sam was there . . . No, not something: I smelled him. He'd taken to using a certain after-shave lotion while he was a man, and it stayed on when he relapsed.

To create a diversion I said to one guard, "Sir—I saw a dog in the Medieval Wing. He had his paws up on the base of the porcelain statuette of St. Sebastian—"

"Oh, my God!"

In a torrent of fear and excitement and thrill, everybody flowed out of the Roman room.

"Sam," I whispered, "Sam—are you here?"

From behind one statue came a very quiet woof. And above the belly of the Reclining Venus, Sam's head appeared.

"Why didn't you stay outside? I think we've found—" Those guards were everywhere. "Get down!" I ordered, under my breath.

"Hey, kid—there's no dog in the Medieval Wing. You sure you haven't seen one in here?"

"A dog?" I got wide-eyed and cutesy and awful. But I had to keep them away from Sam.

"Yeah. A dog."

Fortunately a marble statue of a Roman dog happened to be nearby. "Just him." I grinned impishly.

"Thanks a *lot*!" The guard skulked and stalked out.

"We've got to get you out of here—"

"Mama!—there he is!" Some curious little kid was doing detective work on his own.

The people began to stampede in again.

"Run, Sam!"

Sam did some beautiful broken-field running and got through the crowd. He pretended to be heading for the Renaissance—but at the last minute I thought I saw him dodge off toward Ancient Egypt.

Anyway, the crowd was convinced he was pawing among the Botticellis and the Michelangelos, and that's where they thundered . . . I'm sure that every single one of them was enjoying this chase much more than the art they'd come to see.

I meandered, very casually, toward Ancient Egypt . . . Nobody was there . . . "Sam—?"

"Woof!"—from somewhere behind Bubastis, the cat goddess. She would have been outraged, too, if she'd known that this dog was hiding in back of her granite paws.

"I've got to hide you somewhere safe—"

"Woof!" he agreed.

"But where?" Over against the wall was the marble sarcophagus of the Pharaoh Tut-ankh—I don't remember what. Its marble lid was half off so people could look inside. But they couldn't see anything because it was dark in there. (The mummy was gone, by the way—it had been grave-robbed ages ago.) "It'll have to do."

I lifted Sam up and poured him into the sarcophagus. He grumbled and wiggled—after all, who would want to be stuffed into some old Egyptian king's tomb—but when I got him down into the darkness, after a few suspicious sniffs, he settled in.

"Now *stay* there! And shut up!"

"Woof," he promised quietly.

I went back upstairs—as invisibly as I could.

"Timothy!" Mr. Dickinson and Madame Sosostris were wading around in that carpet as if it were the beach at Riis Park. "This is truly amazing. We've found—"

"The spell, Mr. Dickinson! Did you get the spell?"

"Yes. And also—"

"Recite it, please. In Arabic."

"But in addition to the spell—"

"Hurry, Mr. Dickinson!" I went over to the door, to make sure that no one could watch what was coming.

"Oh, all right. But I don't see why this worthless rhyme should be of such vital interest to you. When I've discovered—"

"Just try." My voice was being practical, but my heart was already into the magic. "Just do me a favor—and try!"

"Very well." Mechanically he recited the spell, to humor my whim.

And Dooley shuddered up out of the carpet—in all his genie regalia. His arms, which had been lifted in fury a thousand years ago, reached down and scooped me up, and he gave me a bear hug to end all bear hugs. No magic in it, either—just strength.

"Little Master Timothy! I thought never to see you again—"

He put me down, and Madame Sosostris, who was bubbling with excitement, too, and dying to get in on our reunion, whacked him on the shoulders and said, "Welcome back, Dooley."

"And this is Mr. Dickin—" I stopped. Because I thought Mr. Dickinson might be about to die.

He was staring at Dooley and shaking like a frightened leaf. He put his hand up over his eyes—as if by not seeing a genie you could make him not be—and the three of us thought he was going to faint. But the scholar got the best of him, and he lowered his hand and said, almost calmly, "You know—I believe I shall give up the study of crockery."

"This is the man who translated the spell for us, Dooley."

"Sayidee," said Dooley. (That means "master" in Arabic.) Then he added, "My everlasting thanks!" And he did a grand obeisance.

"There's *so* much I can learn from you!" The frenzy of knowledge overtook the professor. Not many men have the opportunity of picking a genie's brains. "First of all—"

"Not *now*!" I shouted. "We have to get Sam back into shape."

Dooley lifted his right hand and clicked his fingers . . . Then clicked them again, and his genie's outfit changed into a chauffeur's uniform.

For a minute we waited . . . Nothing happened.

"Did it work?" I worried.

"Behold!" Dooley gestured toward the door.

There was Sam! . . . More hugs. And laughing. And congratulations.

(Sam told us later that he'd suddenly become a man again, stretched out in the sarcophagus. And clothed, too— which was considerate on Dooley's part, since none of the ladies in the museum had to scream or be embarrassed. By moving the lid just a little bit, he'd been able to stand up. But that scared the wits out of a guard who was in the room. He thought the Pharaoh was coming back to life. When he saw that it was only a mortal man, he said, "Hey, what were you doin' inside that sarcophagus?" Sam looked at him coldly and said—it was just in the air that day— "Research.")

We explained to Mr. Dickinson about Mr. Bassinger being my dog, and after a few deep breaths he was able to swallow the truth—having just seen a genie rise out of a rug. "Most extraordinary!" he gulped. But then that child-like pleasure that scholars take in telling you something that they've uncovered came into his voice, and he burbled, "But now I really *must* show you what else is concealed in the carpet. It's a veritable library. You see that green vine—"

"That's the spell—"

"Correct. One line of the verse on each side of the carpet. But *now*—that red line in back of it—even more intricately worked—with those glorious purple leaves—that, too, is writing. And far more difficult to decipher. I've only translated the first few words so far."

"May we hear them, sayidee?" said Dooley softly, trying to damp his excitement down.

Mr. Dickinson squinted into the border. " 'Yet should the—the love-sick fool—surrender the Great Ring—' I don't understand that."

"This ring, sayidee." Dooley held up his left hand. "My Magic and my Immortality are melded together within it."

"Most impressive!"

But Dooley's smile was not at all happy. "From the vantage point of a man, perhaps. Read on, sayidee."

" 'Yet should the love-sick fool surrender the Great Ring —and should some mortal maiden receive the gift from him—as token of his love—thenceforth'—mmm—'thenceforth he shall be even as other men.' "

"The true runes of my release!" burst out Dooley. "Woven around me these centuries! Ah, Wizard, Wizard—" he shook his head, but I think it was in a forgiving way—"in your kindness was always cruelty—in your cruelty always kindness, too."

"Does that mean you can be a man?"

"It does, little master. Indeed it does . . . The life of man—it lasts no longer than the scent of jasmine on the air . . . Yet it is sweet nonetheless."

"It's what you've wanted, though, isn't it?"

"More than the jeweled throne of Haroun Al-Raschid itself! To be *free*, little master—*free* of the bondage of magic and the prison of immortality."

"No question about who the 'mortal maiden' is in this case. Rose would jump at the chance to wear that thing. But will it fit her?—it's awfully big."

"*This* ring fits any finger upon which it is put."

"You better watch out—she'll think that it's an engagement ring."

His grin lit up the whole Al-Hazred room.

"Well, goodbye, everybody," said Sam.

"Where do you think *you're* going?" I demanded.

"Right back to my box. If he calls off my spell." Dooley and I locked eyes with each other. We'd completely forgotten. "You've got to face up to it, Tim. Only one of us can be a man. If he turns human, I turn dog."

"Alas, alas," moaned Dooley. He'd had such hopes. "Halfway between my magic and an animal is where the two of us long to be."

"Mm-mmm—" Mr. Dickinson had kept on reading the rug, while listening to us talk. "You needn't worry about that at all."

"Hey!—wouldn't you worry," barked Sam, "if *you* were—"

"Mr. Bassinger—please! The vine goes on. Just listen to what else it says: 'But let his works be permanent, even should he choose man's lowly fate—' still speaking of the genie, of course—'for I did make him to create great things.' "

"Ah, blessed be his wizardry in the end," said Dooley.

"You mean—*I'm* a great thing?" Sam asked bassetly.

"I think you're great, Sam." I put my arm around his waist.

"No doubt about it," said Madame Sosostris and patted his head.

"Let's go home right away and try it out," I said.

We made an arrangement that Dooley would come over every day and tell Mr. Dickinson all that he wanted to know about Near Eastern archaeology, literature, and architecture—and even crockery, if he was still interested in it. The condition was, however, that the professor should keep his mouth shut, so Dooley wouldn't be annoyed by autograph hunters and other nuisances. To celebrate this bonanza of knowledge that he thought was in store for him, Mr. Dickinson asked Madame Sosostris out for a drink . . . I think it must have been about the first time in thirty years that he'd asked a lady to have a drink.

Good old Madame S.! As she sat down and started to

lace her sneakers, I thought about asking her to come back and watch the climax—if there was one—at Sutton Place. But she seemed so pleased to be asked for the drink that I decided to wait and call her tomorrow. And when I get back next September, I'm going to help her have her breakthrough.

The last thing in the Al-Hazred room was for Dooley to point a finger down toward his former prison cell and command it, "Upon the wall, thou deadly web!" The carpet flew up to its proper position. "And never hold my soul again!"

All the way over to Sutton Place, at first in the taxi, then even more strongly going up in the elevator, as the changes came closer and closer and closer, the three of us shared a sensation of wonder. There was something tremendous about to end—Dooley's magic, after a thousand years—and something risky was going to begin: the two of them, choosing to be men. It was funny and important, and sort of frightening. But nobody wanted to talk about it out loud. We all kept quiet and just drank the feeling of strangeness in.

Until we were in the hall outside Aunt Lucy's door. Dooley stopped, frowned, and put his hand on my shoulder. "My master—think what it is you do."

"Are you getting cold feet?"

"Not I! Oh, not I. But the truth that the Wizard worked

into me compels me to say—you surrender a slave, as I am now, for whom most men would give their lives. When the ring is off my finger—" He jerked his hands open, and something I couldn't see was released. "It bears thought."

So I thought about it . . . I was giving up an awful lot. Sure bets at the race track, automobiles, the latest clothes. In finding Dooley I'd had more luck than any other kid I know . . . But the way I feel about luck is, when you get it, you use it hard. Then you give it back, and you don't try to hog it . . . And exactly the same thing is true of magic.

"My mind's made up. Both of you are on your way." I reached for the buzzer.

But before I could press it, Dooley lifted me up and gave me one last monstrous hug. Sam did, too . . . And that's the last of the hugs, I guess. From now on, it'll have to be man to man—handshakes and things like that.

Maybe not, though. While we were waiting for Rose to open the door, Sam said, "Gosh, I hope I make a go of it!"

"Mr. Bassinger," said Dooley, who was all self-confidence now, "do you love Master Timothy Farr?"

"Of course I love Tim! I love Tim and you and Rose and Lucy—and I think I could almost love anybody."

"Then that will suffice. 'Tis said among the Immortals that love is the practice of humanity. Though difficult—very difficult."

"For Lord's sake!" Rose was goggle-eyed. "The rolling

stone rolls 'round again. Miss Lucy—you've got company."

"Why, Sam—" Aunt Lucy came into the hall—"and Dooley—"

For a moment the air was thick with embarrassed memory of what had happened the night before.

But I took her hand—a little con-job, I admit—and said, "Aunt Lucy, everything is fine. Believe me!—everything is fine."

"Miss Farr," said Sam, "I want to apologize for my—my ungentlemanly conduct."

"Forget it, Sam. We all have our lapses."

"Do we ever!"

"And I'm not Miss Farr—I'm Lucy, as you know. The first time Timmy brought you here you stayed for lunch— Will you do so now? We'll begin again—"

"I'd love to!"

So that took care of them.

"Aunt Lucy," I said, "there's one thing, though—am I going to military school?"

"You're going to any school you'd like to."

"Public." That took care of me. "Rose, Dooley has a present for you. It's—" Then I bit my tongue. It was *his* gift, after all. I was dying to watch him put the ring upon her finger—but I know I've got to curb this tendency to look in on other people's lives. "It's something he'll tell you about himself."

Sam and Aunt Lucy settled into some chatter, Rose went

to set another place at the table, and I, who had suddenly had an idea, said, "Dooley, there is *one* thing I'd like—" My last chance to get it.

We went to my bedroom, and, when I told Dooley, he laughed and said, "Strange. My last act of magic." But he did what I asked . . . We both admired it for a while.

"Master Timothy—" he was on his way to the kitchen, where Rose could be heard humming excitedly—"a record should be kept. I shall tell our scholar Dickinson all that I can recollect from the years in which I served the Wizard— the palaces and mountains and towers. But I fear that as my manhood masters me, my memory will fade. And something also should be preserved of this wondrous summer of parakeets and dogs and men . . . For even great deeds that are done by magic can be forgotten utterly."

So that's what I'm doing—keeping a record . . .

It's way after lunch, and I'm taking a breather . . . I keep looking up at my mirror—my antique American bull's-eye mirror! It may seem small and unimportant—and also a waste of good magic—and it isn't reasonable, I know, but I'm glad that it was Dooley's last deed as a genie . . .

In the kitchen Rose and Dooley are laughing. They practiced a new duet about an hour ago. I think it was something from opera . . . And in the living room Sam is laughing, too. He doesn't sound one bit like a dog. At lunch he was really great. Just as good as Aunt Lucy at filling up pauses and making it all sound interesting. That's a sign of manhood, too, I guess.

In a few days I'm off to the wilds of upstate New York . . . And I'm glad. Now that everything is normal around here, I'm sure that I'll have more fun at camp.

But I'm also pretty positive that I made the right decision—to leave it all up to nature . . . Human nature, that is.

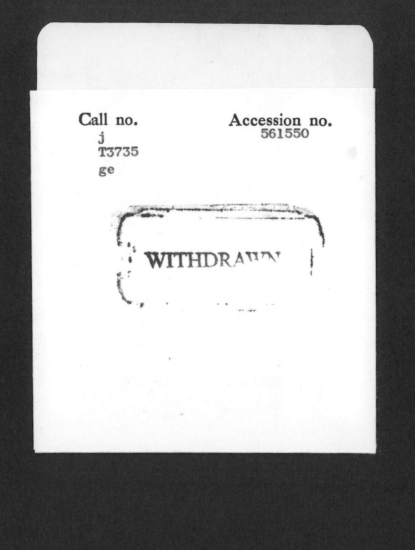